What's All the Fuss About … ?

An Introduction to Doctor Who

For Charlotte

By wishes

Will Hardcastle

What's All the Fuss About ... ?

An Introduction to Doctor Who

By
Will Hadcroft
& Ian Wheeler

FABULOUS BOOKS

www.fbs-publishing.co.uk

First Published in the UK March 2015 by FBS Publishing Ltd.
22 Dereham Road, Thetford,
Norfolk. IP25 6ER

ISBN: 978-0-9932043-0-2

Cover Design by Owen Claxton
Text Edited by Alasdair McKenzie
Typesetting by Jack Rostron

Paper stock used is natural, recyclable and made from wood grown in sustainable
forests. The manufacturing processes conform to environmental regulations.

Dedication

For Mary
– *Ian Wheeler*

&

For Daniel Bentham,
who recently discovered what all the
fuss is about and is totally hooked
– *Will Hadcroft*

CHAPTER 1

THE DOCTOR
As played by
William Hartnell

1963-66

The Doctor is an enigma, a mystery. When he first appeared on television screens in 1963, the viewing public knew nothing about him–his origins, what race he was, what planet he came from–even his name was unknown. Twice in the opening story, characters posed the question 'Doctor who?'

So, Doctor Who isn't the Doctor's name, but rather the name of the series. It is both a question and a statement. The Doctor is a completely unknown entity.

The very first episode, *An Unearthly Child*, sees two secondary school teachers, Ian Chesterton and Barbara Wright, discussing a fifteen-year-old girl named Susan Foreman. They wonder how she could be so intelligent when it came to matters of science and history but woefully ignorant about everyday things such as (in that pre-decimal monetary system era) how many shillings make a pound.

They follow her back to her home, which turns out to be not a house but a junkyard. Susan is nowhere to be seen. Ian and Barbara are curious to find an old police telephone box in the corner of the yard. When Barbara touches it, she is startled to sense a faint vibration.

At that moment, a stern old man with white hair and a Victorian cloak enters the yard. He identifies himself as Susan's grandfather. They know from Susan that he is a doctor of sorts, and address him as 'Doctor Foreman'. An argument erupts when the Doctor refuses to cooperate with them–and then the door of the police box opens and Susan's voice is heard.

Ian is convinced the old man has his granddaughter locked up inside it and, while he struggles with the Doctor, Barbara steps in through the open door.

Stunned by what she sees around her, Barbara freezes. Instead of being in a small space that can accommodate four standing people at best, she is in a huge brightly lit control room. Unknowingly, she has crossed the threshold into another dimension. The Doctor and Ian enter and Susan operates the control that closes the doors.

The ship in which they are standing is the TARDIS, a name Susan made up from the initials of Time And Relative Dimension In Space. The outer shell is disguised as a London police box but will change form when the ship is next moved. It can travel to any planet and to any point in time in that planet's history. The Doctor and Susan are on the run from their own people. Are they refugees fleeing a terrible situation, or criminals escaping justice? There is no way to tell.

Another argument erupts and in the heat of the moment, the Doctor starts the ship. Out of control, the TARDIS leaves 1960s London and materialises in the Stone Age. Upon emerging, the Doctor is dismayed to see that the outer shell is still in the form of a police box. Susan confirms to Ian and Barbara that on previous journeys it has been an ionic column and a sedan chair. But now it appears to have malfunctioned.

The unwilling travellers are then caught between two rival tribes, the leaders of which are desperate to unlock the secret of fire, for not only will it serve them through the oncoming cold spell, but it will also make them powerful in the eyes of their people.

When Ian, Barbara and their mysterious companions escape and reach the safety of the TARDIS, they discover another terrifying truth–the Doctor has no idea how to pilot the ship. It dematerialises from Earth's Stone Age and reappears in a lifeless jungle on the distant future world of Skaro.

And so, the journey for us as viewers begins ...

Who is the Doctor?

We know that the Doctor is from another world. The name of his race and the name of the planet aren't revealed. The reason for him fleeing isn't given. His personal name remains a mystery. We assume he is a scientific doctor, but this isn't explicitly stated.

Prone to wearing black frock coats, flannel trousers and Victorian cloaks, he is very much a man out of time. He doesn't suffer fools, yet there is a tender side to him. While he might place the safety of his friends at risk just to explore an alien city that has aroused his curiosity, he is also fiercely loyal.

The fact that Susan is his granddaughter suggests a family that has been abandoned. Or are they all dead? Presumably the Doctor at one time had a partner and children.

It's an emotional farewell when the Doctor and Susan part company, but he makes no attempt to return to her.

When we later meet another member of his race (see *The Time Meddler*), we still don't find out where either renegade comes from.

Finally, the Doctor is overwhelmed by fatigue. His old body is wearing a bit thin. He collapses in front of his latest travelling companions and undergoes a physical renewal. The cantankerous old man regenerates into a younger-looking person with a craggy face and black hair ...

Try these on DVD!

The Beginning Box Set - comprised of the first three serials;

An Unearthly Child shows us how teachers Ian Chesterton and Barbara Wright become curious about fifteen-year-old Susan Foreman and follow her home to what appears to be a junkyard. There, they confront the Doctor and stumble into the TARDIS. In episodes 2 to 4, the unwilling adventurers are thrown into the Stone Age and have to deal with simple-minded, unreasoning cavemen before escaping back to the ship.

The Daleks picks up immediately where *An Unearthly Child* leaves off. Instead of taking Ian and Barbara back to London 1963, the TARDIS materialises on the future dead planet of Skaro. There, a race of physically perfect and peace-loving people called the Thals are hoping to call upon the mercy of the only other race to survive the nuclear war–the Daleks. But the Daleks are horrible mutations who have retreated into mobile life support units and stay in their metal city. They set out to exterminate the Thals and have their dead world all to themselves.

The set is topped off with the two-part *The Edge of Destruction* and a host of documentary features, including the meticulously researched and captivating *Doctor Who Origins*, which is well worth a look.

The Dalek Invasion of Earth is from the show's second season. The TARDIS lands in London. At first Ian and Barbara think they have finally been returned home. Unfortunately for them it is the year 2164 AD and the Daleks have invaded! They intend to mine out the core of the Earth and pilot the planet like a gigantic spaceship.

Susan becomes romantically involved with freedom fighter, David. After the Daleks are thwarted, the Doctor locks Susan out of the TARDIS and tells her she must settle down with David and have a proper life. With David in her arms, Susan watches the police box fade away.

The Time Meddler is the final story of the second season. Ian and Barbara have at last been returned to 1960s London, and now the Doctor travels with a young woman named Vicki and a space pilot called Steven. The travellers are in England, 1066, and there is a Monk who has somehow come by objects that are anachronistic to the time. He is aware of the significance of the year (the Battle of Hastings and the Normandy conquest of England, for readers outside the UK) and plans to manipulate events to his own ends. When Vicky, and Steven follow the Monk back to his monastery, they witness him emerging from a sarcophagus. Once he is gone, they crawl inside, only to find themselves in a TARDIS ...

The Tenth Planet is known for two firsts–it is the first story to feature the Cybermen and the first story to show the Doctor regenerating into a new persona. It is the future year of 1986 and Earth has come into contact with Mondas, the once tenth planet of our solar system. Its inhabitants have replaced their vital organs and their limbs with cybernetics as a means of self-preservation. When they replaced their flesh and blood brains with computers, they became emotionless Cybermen. Now they seek to turn others into their kind. With the Doctor's help, Earth succeeds in destroying Mondas. But the adventure takes its toll on the Doctor himself. The old man collapses at the controls of the TARDIS, and as Ben and Polly look on, he changes into a younger man.

An Adventure in Space and Time is a docudrama made in 2013 and written by Mark Gatiss in celebration of *Doctor Who*'s fiftieth anniversary. It stars David Bradley as William Hartnell, a middle-aged actor who is sick of playing bad-tempered army sergeants. A twenty-seven-year-old Verity Lambert has been appointed as the producer of a new programme aimed at a family audience, which tells the story of a mysterious time travelling Doctor. She invites Hartnell to take on the role. The programme is a success against the odds and transforms both their lives.

Dr. Who and the Daleks and *Daleks–Invasion Earth 2150 AD* - two full colour cinema feature films based on the first two Dalek serials. Peter Cushing stars as an eccentric human inventor called Dr. Who (in this version he is not an alien on the run from his own people, but an ordinary man, and 'Who' is actually his surname). The Doctor shows off his latest invention, a time travelling police box called *Tardis* to his twelve-year-old granddaughter Susie, his adult granddaughter Barbara and her clumsy boyfriend Ian. Once they have been transported to Skaro, the film takes up the story of the television original. In the second film, Dr. Who and Susie are joined by cousin Louise and policeman Tom (who enters *Tardis* thinking it's a real police box). The film takes up the story of *The Dalek Invasion of Earth*, but thankfully doesn't end with twelve-year-old Susie marrying resistance fighter David!

Miscellany

- While the creation of *Star Trek* is credited to Gene Roddenberry and *Babylon 5* to J Michael Straczynski, there is no on-screen credit for the creators of *Doctor Who*. The basic idea of a mysterious old man known only as 'The Doctor' travelling with human companions through space and time was the brainstorm of BBC Head of Drama, Sidney Newman. He also provided the programme's title. Series 'Bible' writer CE Webber thought up the idea of the Doctor fleeing his own people, a highly advanced alien race from the future. Webber conceptualised the Doctor's ship as a machine that transcends space, time and other dimensions–the outer shell disguising itself as ordinary objects and the interior being vast and existing on a different dimensional plane. Anthony Coburn, the author of the first serial, chose a police telephone box as the ship's initial disguise and came up with the acronym TARDIS. Other key decisions, such as hiring Terry Nation to write the first Dalek serial, were made by producer Verity Lambert and script editor David Whitaker. So, really, Sidney Newman, CE Webber, Anthony Coburn, Verity Lambert and David Whitaker created the core elements of *Doctor Who*.

- The classic run of *Doctor Who* was a series of serials. An adventure would be split into a number of weekly episodes, usually around twenty-five minutes in length. Up until Season Three's *The Savages*, each individual episode of *Doctor Who* had its own title. The very first serial was four episodes in length. From documents discovered in the 1990s it came to light that the production team knew the serial by the overall title *100,000 BC*. However, this never appeared on screen, and to most fans the serial has always been known by its episode 1 title *An Unearthly Child*. From *The Savages* onwards, the production team began giving one title to a whole serial, with the episodes numbered. For example, the Doctor's regeneration took place in *The Tenth Planet* episode 4.

• The theme music for the programme was composed by Ron Grainer. Rather than get Grainer to have a small TV orchestra record the theme, as was usually the custom, the composition was given to Delia Derbyshire at the BBC Radiophonic Workshop to realise it electronically by synchronising a number of reel-to-reel tape recorders. Grainer was so astounded by the ethereal quality of the end result he wanted Delia to have half his royalty and be credited on screen. Sadly, due to union rules at the time, Delia received neither. On screen, the theme music was credited to 'Ron Grainer and the BBC Radiophonic Workshop'. In time, Delia Derbyshire left the BBC and worked for British Gas. Only after her death was she recognised beyond *Doctor Who* fandom as a pioneer of electronic music.

• The TARDIS was originally meant to change form to blend in with whatever landscape it found itself in. Writer Anthony Coburn chose a police telephone box for the first episode. When it became clear that the series had been assigned a pitifully low budget, the production team saved some money by having the TARDIS malfunction and get stuck as a police box. The interior of the ship was designed by Peter Brachacki. He reportedly threw together the white walls with their circular indentations and the six-sided console swiftly because he felt the series was beneath him. Ironically, it is now regarded as one of the most innovative spaceship interiors in television history.

- The noise that the TARDIS makes when it dematerialises was created by Brian Hodgson at the BBC Radiophonic Workshop. He scraped his mother's Yale front door key down the bass string of an old piano and treated the sound electronically.

- Police boxes were a common sight on street corners throughout the 1950s and 1960s. The TARDIS type was particularly common in London. The purpose of the box was to serve as a mini police station. The officer could go inside and eat his lunch or lock a criminal in it until a patrol car turned up. The telephone wasn't in the box itself but was housed in a panel on the left-hand door. It was accessible to the public. The lamp on top flashed if the main station wanted to contact the officer. When the walkie-talkie radio found its way onto the beat, the days of the police box were numbered. By the late 1970s most had been removed from Britain's streets. In the 1990s the Metropolitan Police fought the BBC to own the rights to the design, but lost the case when the court decreed that, to the public, the police box *was* the TARDIS!

- The Daleks in Terry Nation's debut script were said to be pepper pot shaped, carried strange weapons in their hands and had a lens suspended on a stalk on their domed heads. He wanted his alien not to look human at all, not to be obviously a man dressed up in a costume. Designer Raymond Cusick came up with an intricate design, but was told that the show's budget would only allow one prop to be made. Cusick simplified the design, staying with the pepper pot shape but substituting the calliper-like hands with a sink plunger. Nation went on to make a lot of money as the inventor of the Daleks, while Cusick received the standard BBC designer's fee. The Nazi-like delivery of the Dalek voices was developed by actor Peter Hawkins.

- In 1966, producer Innes Lloyd wanted a new regular enemy for the Doctor to battle against, as he felt the Daleks had made too many appearances. Script editor Gerry Davis and science writer Kit Pedler created the Cybermen, a race of human-like beings who had become so riddled with disease from the pollution on their planet that they'd replaced their limbs and vital organs with plastic and metal equivalents. They symbolised Pedler's concerns about what we were doing to our own world, and where advances in cybernetics might take us.

- The concept of the Doctor regenerating into a different-looking man with an altered persona was not there from the programme's inception. Neither Head of Drama Sydney Newman, treatment writer CE Webber, producer Verity Lambert nor script editor

David Whitaker (the collective creators of the show) had any inkling of the idea. It came about three years later when actor William Hartnell became too ill to continue in the role of the Doctor. Head of Drama Sean Sutton and producer Innes Lloyd had a choice–cancel *Doctor Who* after Season Four, or find a way to continue without William Hartnell. Initially, they looked for actors who might play a younger version of Hartnell, so they could say the Doctor had been rejuvenated. Michael Horden was approached, an actor similar in performance style to Hartnell, but he turned it down. When Patrick Troughton agreed, it was with a proviso–he wouldn't be playing a rejuvenated Hartnell, but rather he would reinterpret the role his own way. Had viewers rejected the redefining of the Doctor, the series would have been cancelled at the end of that season in 1966. However, the audience embraced the change, and not only did *Doctor Who* continue, but a precedent had been set.

• Before the advent of home video, the BBC had a policy of screening a programme once, followed by a repeat maybe later in the year, and then wiping the tape to make room in their archives. In the late 1960s and for a further decade, the BBC wiped tapes regardless of what was on them. As a result, around 97 individual black-and-white episodes of *Doctor Who* have been lost. It was done indiscriminately, too, meaning that while entire serials are now gone, quite a few remaining stories are incomplete. For example, the final episode of *The Tenth Planet* is still missing, except for the Doctor's regeneration, which was used in an episode of children's magazine programme *Blue*

Peter (which wasn't wiped!). For the DVD release, the soundtrack of the episode was obtained from a fan who had taped it off-air at the time of broadcast. They cleaned it up and synchronised it with black-and-white animation. The clip of the original live action regeneration is featured on the disc as an extra. Some stories were saved from destruction by fans that worked at the BBC at the time– such as the very first Dalek serial, which was found bundled up and ready burn. Thankfully, fan Ian Levine did the decent thing and took it home.

CHAPTER 2

THE DOCTOR
As played by
Patrick Troughton

1966-69

If we think we know the Doctor by the time the Cybermen make their debut, that sense of familiarity evaporates when he undergoes his first bodily renewal—a complete change of physical appearance resulting in a scrambled personality.

The Second Doctor is shorter, younger looking, with a mess of dark hair and a craggy face. The black frock coat is now a size too big. His shirt is crumpled, a bow tie was attached with a safety pin, and his half mast trousers are held up with rope.

While the Doctor's original persona was short-tempered and cantankerous, this new one is warmer, cheery and at times quite comical.

When he first sits up and examines his altered face, his companions Ben and Polly are huddled in a corner of the TARDIS control room, wondering how this man can be the same Doctor. As their adventures with him unfold, they see he is still driven to respond to injustices and motivated to protect the underdog. He is the same man.

As his travelling companions come and go, the Doctor is content to drift from one situation to another. He has no control over the TARDIS and doesn't care. When his orphaned friend Victoria needs reassurance, he tells her he keeps his own family and loved ones alive in his memory. He may appear to be a cosmic hobo, but he is in possession of a sharp intellect.

Who is the Doctor?

We still know nothing of the Doctor's origins until he finds himself caught in a blend of time zones where various armies from Earth's past are encouraged to war with one another. An alien race of War Lords has procured knowledge of time travel technology from another humanoid alien promoted to the position of War Chief. He recognises the Doctor. The two renegades are of the same world–they have fled from the society of Time Lords. The War Chief is aware that the Doctor has changed his appearance since they last met. The Doctor insists he had every right to leave the Time Lords.

The situation with the War Lords is out of control, their plan to form the ultimate galactic army insane. The Doctor is left with no option but to call upon his own people to intervene, knowing that doing so will expose his own location in space and time. The Time Lords put a stop to the war games and capture the Doctor.

We learn that he was bored with Time Lord society; they hardly ever used their great powers to help others in need. He wasn't content to just observe other worlds and times, and 'borrowed' the TARDIS to explore the universe. His actions contravened their First Law of Time, and called for the death sentence.

In his defence, the Doctor accuses the Time Lords of being morally inept for not using their abilities to help races in dire straits. He has battled the likes of the Quarks, the Yeti, the Macra, the Cybermen and the Daleks.

Softened by the Doctor's plea, the Time Lord court annuls the death sentence and chooses instead to exile him to twentieth-century Earth. When he protests that he is known on Earth and may become a target, the Time Lords enforce another change of appearance and send him on his way ...

Try these on DVD!

The Tomb of the Cybermen sees the Doctor, his companion Jamie from eighteenth-century Scotland and their newly acquired friend from Victorian England, Victoria, arrive on the planet Telos to find an expedition party attempting to gain entry into an ice tomb in which Cybermen are in suspended animation. But who among the expedition have their own agenda?

The Enemy of the World - The TARDIS takes the Doctor and his companions to Earth's future, where a politician named Salamander is manipulating natural phenomena and the business world in order to seize rulership of the world. An underground movement is poised to stop him. Their greatest weapon? A man who looks exactly like him–the Doctor.

In *The Web of Fear* the TARDIS gets caught in a web-like substance active in Earth's vicinity. The ship materialises in the London underground train network, where the Great Intelligence is using robot Yeti to subdue the human race. The British army squadron dispatched to help the Doctor is led by Colonel Alistair Gordon Lethbridge-Stewart.

In *The Mind Robber* the TARDIS literally falls apart! While Jamie and new space-age computer genius Zoe cling to the floating console for dear life, the Doctor drifts into oblivion. The three travellers meet up in a bizarre Land of Fiction, where they encounter characters like Gulliver from Jonathan Swift's *Gulliver's Travels* and a unicorn. But who is creating the story they are trapped in, and for what purpose?

The Invasion sees the Doctor, Jamie and Zoe on contemporary Earth. They are investigating businessman Tobias Vaughn and his Electromatics company. In London's sewers a new grade of Cybermen await his signal to awake and invade. Meanwhile, the Doctor and his companions are aided by the newly formed United Nations Intelligence Taskforce (UNIT), headed by Alistair Lethbridge-Stewart, who has been promoted from Colonel to Brigadier. Episodes 1 and 4 of this eight-part story are missing from the BBC's archives. For the DVD release, the soundtrack is synchronised with animations created by the award-winning Cosgrove Hall Productions.

The War Games is an epic adventure in which alien War Lords are bent on gathering armies from different time zones to create the ultimate military organisation. They are employing as War Chief a member of the Doctor's own race, who is supplying them with time travel technology. We discover the Doctor is from a society of highly advanced Time Lords and that he stole the TARDIS to go on his travels. In so doing he became involved in the affairs of other worlds, thus breaking the cardinal rule of his own people. In his defence the Doctor charges the Time Lords with negligence, with failing to use their knowledge and powers to help those in need. The death sentence is quashed and he faces an enforced physical change and banishment to twentieth-century Earth.

Miscellany

- William Hartnell handed over the role of the Doctor to Patrick Troughton at the end of the second story in

26

Season Four, 1966. Troughton completely redefined the persona of the character, making him more impish and comedic. Had the audience rejected the new characterisation, *Doctor Who* would have been cancelled at the end of the season. However, the renewal of the Doctor brought revitalisation for the series as a whole, and it enjoyed continued success.

• The Second Doctor's first story was *The Power of the Daleks*, a tale wiped in its entirety from the BBC's archives, save for one or two brief clips. Thanks to a fan recording the soundtrack off-air on reel-to-reel tape, the BBC was able to release the adventure with linking narration on audio CD. Later, they put out a new version synchronised with photographs taken on set which can be played picture strip-style on a home computer. Fans are hoping a full animation will be released on DVD.

• The fourth adventure in the season, *The Highlanders*, would be the final purely historical (non-science fiction) story to be produced until 1982's *Black Orchid*. Sydney Newman's vision for the series, that it would be part educational, had all but evaporated by now. This story introduced Frazer Hines as the kilt-wearing Jacobite Scot, Jamie. It wasn't until Hines left *Doctor Who* that most viewers realised his Scottish accent was fake.

• Producer Innes Lloyd commissioned a new title sequence from graphic designer Bernard Lodge. It continued the 'waves of time' theme from the previous version, but now had the series logo in

Times New Roman font rather than Arial and the Doctor's face coming through the mist (an effect vetoed by original series producer Verity Lambert, because she felt that William Hartnell's stern face would frighten the younger viewers).

- Delia Derbyshire, who had created the programme's theme music from Ron Grainer's composition, was hired to add a few more bars to the rhythm and some extra sounds to the mix to make it heavier.

- Innes Lloyd had Gerry Davis as his script editor, and Davis's friend Dr Kit Pedler as a scientific advisor to the show. Davis and Pedlar developed their Cybermen idea throughout the Troughton era.

- Innes Lloyd wanted the Daleks written out of the series permanently, as he felt they had run their course. Original series script editor David Whitaker was hired to write the Terry Nation-approved *The Evil of the Daleks*, in which the metal fascists, along with their Emperor (making its debut in the series), are completely wiped out.

- The Doctor uses a device called the sonic screwdriver for the first time in *Fury From the Deep*. It emits high-frequency sound waves to disrupt electronic apparatus. The Doctor uses it to dismantle equipment and unlock doors.

- By the time Lloyd and Davis had handed the show over to Peter Bryant and Derrick Sherwin in 1968, the series was beginning to decline in audience appreciation. Viewing figures were dropping and the BBC were looking for ways to save money. Bryant and Sherwin suggested restricting the Doctor to contemporary Earth so as not to spend money on futuristic sets and costumes. The concept was tried out on *The Invasion*, introducing UNIT as a team that could help the Doctor. The story was a ratings success. When Patrick Troughton announced his resignation in 1969, the BBC considered cancelling the series at the end of its current run.

- Incoming script editor Terrance Dicks was called upon to explain some of the Doctor's origins in the final story *The War Games*, just in case the show was cancelled. He and fellow writer Malcolm Hulke came up with the concept of the Time Lords. When the Doctor is exiled to Earth and a new regeneration is enforced upon him, we don't get to see who Patrick Troughton turns into–as it still wasn't certain there would be another series.

CHAPTER 3

THE DOCTOR
As played by
Jon Pertwee

1970-74

Dashing and heroic, the Third Doctor is a man of action and, with his love of flamboyant clothes, a dandy. With a passion for fast vehicles and gadgetry, he is arguably more akin to the famous fictional secret agent James Bond 007 than the eccentric professor and clown that his predecessors had been. This heroic figure is an expert in Venusian karate, a master swordsman, and loves to dress in stylish velvet capes and smoking jackets. He also enjoys the finer things in life, such as a good cheese or wine.

Exiled by the Time Lords, the Third Doctor is forced to live on Earth for much of his lifespan, and whilst he often finds the people of our world to be frustrating, he nonetheless cares deeply for the human race. In particular, he builds up a strong friendship with Alistair Gordon Lethbridge-Stewart, now a Brigadier and in charge of the British arm of the United Nations Intelligence Taskforce (UNIT), which has been set up to protect Earth from alien menaces, mad scientists and other strange happenings.

The Third Doctor develops strong relationships with his three human companions. His first assistant, Dr Elizabeth Shaw, is almost the Doctor's intellectual equal. With his second companion, Jo Grant, the Doctor is very much a mother hen figure, providing protection and reassurance during their travels. Finally, he meets Sarah Jane Smith, a feisty journalist who will prove to be one of the Time Lord's longest-lasting friends.

This Doctor is an expert at techno-jargon and becomes famous for his catchphrase 'Reverse the polarity of the neutron flow,' although in fact he only says this twice! Being based on Earth, the new Doctor needs a more terrestrial form of transport in the shape of Bessie, his distinctive yellow Edwardian roadster.

Who is the Doctor?

Banished to Earth by his own people, the Third Doctor becomes mankind's protector during a period of sustained attempts by various alien races and unscrupulous humans to conquer the planet. At first the Doctor seems displeased by the altered appearance the Time Lords have given him, but he grows to like it and creates a new image for himself using clothes taken from a doctor's changing room in a hospital. For the first time, we learn that our hero has two hearts. The Doctor once again meets Brigadier Lethbridge-Stewart, who at first does not believe the Time Lord is the same man as the one he has previously encountered during incidents involving the Yeti and Cybermen.

To begin with, the Time Lords largely leave the Doctor alone as he defeats alien menaces and Earth-based dangers. Then, a fellow Time Lord in a business suit and bowler hat warns the Doctor that he will re-encounter his old enemy the Master, who the Doctor had once been friends with. The Doctor and the Master clash several times and the Master is ultimately imprisoned by UNIT, although he subsequently escapes.

When the Doctor's home planet is threatened by Omega, the stellar engineer who created the supernova that powers Time Lord civilisation, the Time Lords bring back the Doctor's two past incarnations to help him. When the Doctors defeat Omega, the Time Lords once again allow the Third Doctor the freedom of time and space.

Following an incident involving terrifying giant maggots, the Doctor's companion Jo leaves him, as she has fallen in love with the environmentalist Professor

Clifford Jones. The Doctor's pain at losing her is clear to see. Fortuitously, he soon encounters journalist Sarah Jane Smith, who will also become a hugely important part of his life.

After defeating the hideous alien spider called the Great One, the Doctor absorbs a deadly dose of radiation and, assisted by the Time Lord Cho-Je, regenerates.

This incarnation of the Doctor claims to have been a scientist for thousands of years, but as this is at odds with comments made by the other Doctors, it may well be that he is simply showing off! He also remembers living on top of a mountain when he was a little boy and meeting a hermit who told him the secret of life. Also during this incarnation, the Doctor reveals he cannot simply do as he wishes when he is time travelling–during an adventure involving the Daleks, he tells Jo about a scientific principle called the Blinovitch Limitation Effect, which means a time traveller cannot cross his own timestream.

Try these on DVD!

In *Spearhead From Space*, what appear to be meteorites bring the Nestene Consciousness to Earth. This alien presence is able to manipulate anything made of plastic. Cue shop window mannequins coming to life and attacking pedestrians on the high street! Key humans have been kidnapped and copied. Meanwhile, the newly regenerated and exiled Doctor tumbles out of the TARDIS. He reluctantly agrees to help the Brigadier and UNIT combat unusual menaces in exchange for a laboratory and equipment so he may escape his exile and resume his travels. First up–he must defeat the Nestene

Consciousness and the Autons. (This and *Terror of the Autons* are available in the box set *Mannequin Mania*).

Doctor Who and the Silurians - A nuclear research centre on Wenley Moor is experiencing power drainage. Members of staff are suffering mental breakdowns. UNIT is called in to investigate. One of the workers has been clawed to death by a creature in the caves. The Doctor and Liz go to check it out, only to discover a dinosaur! Deep beneath the research centre a race of reptilian bipeds are waking from suspended animation and they seem to think the Earth is theirs. Written by Malcolm Hulke, this is the first of many Pertwee-era stories to consider ecological issues, man's immaturity and short-sightedness and his ruination of the planet.

Inferno is a much-loved tale about scientists in a research centre endeavouring to drill to the centre of the Earth. There are concerns that the project may release unknown forces. Some toxic gas mutates one of the workers into a primordial beast, and attempts by the Doctor to use the research centre's facilities to restore the TARDIS so he can escape his exile throw him into a parallel dimension where UNIT is subject to a totalitarian government, and where the Brigadier is the Brigade Leader, Liz Shaw is a Section Leader and Sergeant Benton is Platoon Under Leader Benton. In this reality, the project is closer to completion and the Earth is doomed.

Terror of the Autons introduces new companion Jo Grant and the Doctor's arch Time Lord rival The Master, who possesses his own fully functional TARDIS and a weapon that shrinks its victims down to doll-sized corpses. Having acquired the last remaining cell of the Nestene Consciousness, the Master is building a new army of Autons to do his bidding. The Doctor and Jo must confront a living plastic troll doll, bogus policemen, a killer chair and a deadly telephone cord in their battle to stop him.

The Daemons is considered to be the archetypal Third Doctor story by those who worked on the series at the time. In the village of Devil's End, an archaeological dig is excavating a Bronze Age burial mound called the Devil's Hump. The local white witch, Olive Hawthorne, warns of the coming of the horned beast. Sure enough, the Master is masquerading as the local vicar and is determined to summon up the demonic Azal in the cavern below the church. This is a superb example of a UNIT story, with all the regular cast members in place, and a great appearance by Roger Delgado as the original incarnation of the Master.

Day of the Daleks marks the first appearance in the television series of the Daleks in colour. Sir Reginald Styles is holding peace talks with the world's major rulers at his manor house. They are hoping to broker a deal that will stave off the threat of World War Three. Guerrilla soldiers from the future come back in time with the intention of killing Styles, as their history records he sabotaged the peace process, which allowed the Daleks to invade the crippled society which survived the ensuing war. Gaining The Doctor and Jo travel to the future where they encounter the human race slaving under the yoke of the Daleks. But who really enabled the invasion to take place? (In the *Special Edition* box set, there is the story as originally broadcast and a re-edited version with new CGI effects and sounds, new Dalek voices by Nicholas Briggs, and specially shot sequences in which more Daleks are added to the battle sequence to make it look more convincing. This release is highly recommended).

The Curse of Peladon sees the return of the Ice Warriors, a popular reptilian foe from the Troughton era. The Doctor and Jo arrive on the planet Peladon which, under the leadership of its young King, is about to join the Galactic Federation, and the two time travellers are mistaken for delegates from Earth. The High Priest Hepesh does not want Peladon to be part of the Federation and warns that the curse of Aggedor, the Royal Beast of Peladon, will bring doom to them all. It transpires that there is indeed something big and furry lurking in the tunnels beneath the citadel. Can the Doctor tame the beast and help prevent Hepesh from returning the planet to its days of isolationism and superstition? And which of the delegates is in league with Hepesh to sabotage the conference? This story is available as part of the *Peladon Tales* boxset with its sequel *The Monster of Peladon*.

In *The Three Doctors*, the Doctor needs help from the Time Lords when a strange blob of energy seems intent on capturing him. With their own crisis involving a black hole to deal with, the Time Lords send the Doctor's first and second incarnations to assist him. When the First Doctor realises the black hole is a bridge between universes, the Second and Third Doctors travel into a strange anti-matter universe and meet the originator of time travel, Omega. Look out for kooky monsters called

Gel Guards and enjoy the great chemistry between the Second and Third Doctors, with both Patrick Troughton and Jon Pertwee on top form.

Carnival of Monsters - is a quirky, unusual story which is well worth a look. Vorg, a travelling showman, wanders the galaxy with his Miniscope, a device which contains miniaturised versions of various aliens such as Daleks and Cybermen to show to spectators. Meanwhile, the Doctor and Jo land on the *SS Bernice*, a cargo ship that mysteriously disappeared in the Indian Ocean in 1926. But why does a hatch in the ship, invisible to the crew, lead inexplicably to futuristic corridors and marsh lands, where the two friends encounter ferocious monsters called Drashigs? And how are the events happening to the Doctor and Jo linked to the Miniscope?

The Green Death - The Doctor and UNIT investigate the mysterious death of a miner in an abandoned Welsh coal mine. The nearby Global Chemicals oil plant claims to be able to produce more petrol and diesel from crude oil than other processes but create less waste, leading the Brigadier to suspect a link between the plant and the man's death. Jo finds a lake of strange green slime in the mine tunnels, filled with giant maggots. What is the secret of Global Chemicals and what are the intentions of its supercomputer, BOSS?

This story is notable for its ecological themes, something that was close to the heart of producer Barry Letts.

The Time Warrior introduces Sarah Jane Smith and the alien warmongering clone race the Sontarans. The

Doctor and Sarah travel back to the Middle Ages, where they find King Irongron and his men doing business with Sontaran commander Linx, who is trying to repair his spaceship. In order to get what he wants, Linx must help Irongron develop weapons to defeat a neighbouring kingdom. A lighthearted romp, this story is worth watching for the sparring between the two military minds (Irongron and Linx) as each struggles to tolerate the demands of the other.

In *Death to the Daleks,* both the Doctor and the Daleks land on the planet Exxilon. The TARDIS and the Dalek ship are drained of power and the Daleks have to use machine guns instead of their more usual energy blasters! In order to escape, the Doctor must venture into the Exxilon City, where he must avoid traps and solve a variety of puzzles and challenges. His mission–to destroy the City's beacon, the cause of the energy drain. He's going to need his wits–and the help of the Daleks– to do it. But the City's computer brain has other ideas and creates weird 'antibodies' to stop him ...

Miscellany

- Jon Pertwee was the *Doctor Who* production team's second choice for the Third Doctor after actor Ron Moody had turned the role down. Pertwee decided on the Doctor's image himself after wearing some of his grandfather's old clothes for a photo shoot.

- Pertwee's first season was much shorter than those of his predecessors. Hartnell and Troughton been on screen for most of the year, with only a few weeks' break. Pertwee's first series was only twenty-five weeks long. This, along with confining the Doctor to Earth, was part of an attempt by the BBC to decrease the cost of making the series. *Doctor Who* did, however, have the bonus of being in colour for the first time, and this allowed the BBC to utilise the new Colour Separation Overlay technique, which allowed actors to be shown against any background the producers chose.

• A new title sequence was introduced for Pertwee's first story. The sequence utilised the 'howl-around' technique used for the previous opening titles, but as the method did not produce satisfactory results when used with colour equipment, the titles were produced in black and white and then tinted with colour.

• The Third Doctor's first adventure, *Spearhead from Space*, was the first *Doctor Who* story to be made entirely on location and entirely on film, whereas the series' stories were normally a mix of film for location work and videotape in the studio. This was due to industrial action by members of staff at the BBC. The only other *Doctor Who* story to be made entirely on film would be the *Doctor Who* TV movie in 1996.

• As Pertwee's first season progressed, producer Barry Letts and script editor Terrance Dicks observed how the relationship between the Doctor and Brigadier Lethbridge-Stewart was like that of Sherlock Holmes and Dr Watson. What the Doctor now needed, they decided, was a Moriarty figure, an arch rival. They knew this character would be a Time Lord, would have his own TARDIS and would be as ingenious as the Doctor. Dicks considered how the series' protagonist had adopted an academic title. The next grade up from a doctorate was a master's degree. Dicks suggested that the Doctor's nemesis should be called The Master.

- Actor Nicholas Courtney, who played Brigadier Lethbridge-Stewart, often joked that UNIT was the most seriously undermanned military operation in the world, headed as it was only by the Brigadier, Captain Yates and Sergeant Benton.

- Robert Holmes had scripted a couple of Second Doctor serials and was favoured by script editor Terrance Dicks. Once the Third Doctor's earthbound series had been defined, Holmes was able to indulge his love of the macabre. He created the Autons, which were an immediate hit with the audience, and gave the Master his nuances and ingenuity. The programme was adopting a more adult tone and as a result was saved from cancellation. The downside was that the show came in for heavy criticism, not least from Scotland Yard, who asked producer Barry Letts not to make policemen look frightening. After this, Letts softened the tone of the series.

- The role of King Peladon in *The Curse of Peladon* was played by David Troughton, son of Second Doctor Patrick Troughton. David had appeared alongside his father in *The War Games* in 1969 and would return to the series in 2008 for the David Tennant story *Midnight*.

- Innes Lloyd had commissioned what was meant to be the last ever Dalek serial in 1967 (*The Evil of the Daleks*). Letts and Dicks had no great desire to bring them back. But when BBC Managing Director Huw Wheldon asked when the Daleks were coming back, they realised the metal fascists could be added to Louis Marks' script about guerrilla soldiers travelling back in time from the far future to prevent World War Three. The amended script became *Day of the Daleks*.

- The *Doctor Who* production team had hoped that First Doctor William Hartnell would be able to play a bigger role in *The Three Doctors*. Unfortunately, as Hartnell was now quite ill and frail, he was unable to participate in the studio sessions and his participation was reduced to a pre-recorded cameo role (made at the BBC's Ealing Studios) which showed him appearing on the TARDIS scanner. The three Doctors did all get together for a promotional photo shoot.

- Actor Roger Delgado, who played the Master, tragically died in a car crash in Turkey in 1973 when the car he was travelling in went off the road into a ravine. Jon Pertwee would often say that Delgado's death was one of the reasons he left the series in 1974. It had been intended that the Third Doctor's final adventure, provisionally entitled *The Final Game*, would have been the ultimate showdown between the Doctor and the Master, who would have been revealed to be brothers.

- The Third Doctor's most futuristic form of transport was the 'Whomobile' a flying car which appeared in the stories *Invasion of the Dinosaurs* and *Planet of the Spiders*. The car actually belonged to Jon Pertwee, who had had it custom built. The vehicle was made of fibreglass and was fourteen feet long, seven feet across and had fins that reached five feet into the air. The vehicle, also known as 'The Alien', was not referred to by name in the series.

- For Season Ten, graphic designer Bernard Lodge was invited to create a brand new title sequence. Utilising the then state-of-the-art technique called slit-scan, he replaced the kaleidoscope 'howl-around' effect with a 'time tunnel', the Doctor's face coming through a mist, and a diamond-shaped logo creating a tunnel of its own.

- It isn't until the tenth season story *The Time Warrior* that the Doctor's home planet is named 'Gallifrey'.

- Pertwee would return to play the Doctor again for the twentieth anniversary special *The Five Doctors* in 1983, on stage in a production called *The Ultimate Adventure* in 1989, and on radio for two adventures, *The Paradise of Death* in 1993 and *The Ghosts of N-Space* in 1996.

- The Pertwee era saw the launch of the *Doctor Who* Target books, a series of novelisations of the *Doctor Who* stories. Beginning with reprints of three stories which had previously been released in the 1960s, the range lasted for many years, and virtually every televised story would ultimately be novelised. Pre-home video, these were the only way a fondly remembered *Doctor Who* serial could be enjoyed again. The books were a publishing phenomenon, selling millions of copies, and would help many a young *Doctor Who* fan learn to read!

• Sarah Jane Smith, played by Elisabeth Sladen, was to prove to be one of the Doctor's most popular companions with the viewing public and the longest-serving.

CHAPTER 4

THE DOCTOR
As played by
Tom Baker

1974-81

The Doctor's fourth incarnation starts as a bewildered eccentric, his brain scrambled by the regeneration process. Eager to cement his new independence from the Time Lords, he only accepts a commission because they want him to prevent the creation of his deadliest enemy, and he cannot resist. After that, he is intent on being free.

The regeneration causes the Doctor to lose his sense of home with the Brigadier and UNIT, choosing to stay away for longer and longer periods until he severs all ties.

Beneath the otherworldly, eccentric idiosyncrasies is a serious brooding genius. In time he becomes frivolous, taking his enemies in his stride and laughing up his sleeve at their threats. Nothing seems to faze him. But as the stakes get to the point where the existence of the whole universe is threatened, the Doctor's casual approach gives way to a dark and sombre mood. He must stop his arch nemesis if it is the last thing he does.

Who is the Doctor?

With a tangle of brown hair, bewildered, staring blue eyes, a frock coat, an immensely long multicoloured scarf and a broad-brimmed hat, the Doctor is eager to get back in the TARDIS and roam through the cosmos. His companion Sarah Jane loves his free spirit; they are the best of friends. He explains that she can hear alien languages in English thanks to a Time Lord gift he shares with her telepathically.

The Doctor states to an adversary who knows his origins that he has renounced Time Lord society and is now merely a wanderer in time and space. He is seven hundred and fifty years old. When recalled to Gallifrey, he must send Sarah home—what lies ahead is not for her.

We learn a little of his personal history–he was once a student of Lord Borusa in the Prydonian chapter of the Academy. We see the Doctor donning Time Lord robes and challenging his old enemy The Master, who has now reached the end of his thirteenth and final life and is desperate to tap into dark Gallifreyan secrets to renew himself.

The Doctor isn't keen to stay on his home world any longer than absolutely necessary, and is soon on his way again. Later, he is joined by a primitive woman named Leela and endeavours to civilise her. The pair accept the gift of a mobile computer in the form of a robot dog: K9.

When Leela has gone, the Doctor is assigned by the Guardian of Light in Time–or the White Guardian–to find and assemble the six pieces of the Key to Time. He is given an assistant from his own world, a woman named Romanadvoratrelundar–Romana for short. After the Key has been assembled and the balance between good and evil has been restored, Romana regenerates into a new persona. The Doctor takes it in his stride. After all, she is one of his own people.

But then, Gallifrey wants her back. She chooses to stay in the 'pocket universe' of E-Space; she takes K9 with her.

Upon returning to N-Space ('Normal Space', i.e. our universe), the Doctor and his new friend Adric are summoned to the paradise world of Traken by its Keeper. A malevolent sentient statue has rooted itself in the grove and is intent on seizing the power of the Keepership. The Doctor discovers that the statue is a kind of TARDIS and that its occupant is known to him.

And then his arch rival unwittingly unleashes entropy into the universe–the universe which has long passed the point of total collapse. The Doctor and the newly regenerated Master must join forces to halt it, but can our hero trust his old enemy not to turn traitor on him at the first opportunity?

Try These on DVD!

Tom Baker played the Doctor for seven years, in which time the series was overseen by four different producers, each with his particular preferences in tone and style. Barry Letts (Jon Pertwee's producer) made Baker's debut story. Philip Hinchcliffe favoured a gothic flavour, while Graham Williams went for light entertainment, and John Nathan-Turner (who produced Baker's final season) elected to move the programme away from the whimsical to hard science.

Under Producer Philip Hinchcliffe (1974-77)

Pre-dating Ridley Scott's *Alien* movie by four years, *The Ark in Space* is a serious science fiction tale. Far off in the future, after Earth has been bombarded by solar flares, an orbiting space station carries the remnants of the human race cryogenically frozen in suspended animation. When the TARDIS brings the Doctor, Sarah and UNIT medic Harry Sullivan on board, the Doctor marvels at the indomitable nature of Homo sapiens. But when the station's commander is revived, it isn't long before he starts to behave erratically, and his body undergoes a metamorphosis. The Ark has been invaded by an alien parasite.

Genesis of the Daleks - The Doctor, Sarah and Harry have their transmat beam diverted, so that instead of arriving back at the TARDIS they materialise on Skaro at a point in time where the humanoid Kaleds and Thals have been at war for a thousand years. The Time Lords commission the Doctor to try and prevent the creation of his deadliest enemies, or at the very least affect their development so that they become less aggressive creatures. In the Kaled bunker, the Doctor encounters Davros for the very first time–a crippled scientist seated in a wheelchair resembling the base of a Dalek. Davros has created a mobile life support-system for the creature his race will ultimately mutate into–the Daleks. But he has perverted their genetic development so they are devoid of conscience, regarding themselves as the supreme beings. However, Davros has not accounted for one fundamental truth–he himself is not a Dalek ...

In *Terror of the Zygons*, the Doctor, Sarah and Harry are recalled to Earth to investigate the destruction of oil rigs off the Scottish coast. Something huge appears to have bitten chunks out of the foundations. Shape-shifting aliens are impersonating key figures to ensure control of the human race. Highly atmospheric, this is the last story to regularly feature Brigadier Lethbridge-Stewart.

In *Pyramids of Mars* the TARDIS is drawn off course and materialises in a manor house in 1911. It is the home of Marcus Scarman, an expert in Egyptology who has brought back a mysterious sarcophagus. But Scarman is not himself; he has been taken over by Sutekh, an alien god imprisoned on Mars. The Doctor and Sarah join forces with Marcus's brother Lawrence and have to battle robot mummies to stop Scarman releasing the ancient evil that is Sutekh.

The Seeds of Doom starts off at the Antarctic and then unfolds in an English country house. Millionaire botanist Harrison Chase learns of an alien pod that has fallen to Earth. He has it brought to his home. Chase cares more about plants than he does people and will stop at nothing to protect and nurture the lethal Krynoid.

The Deadly Assassin sees the Doctor returning to Gallifrey alone, having experienced a premonition in which the President of the Time Lords is assassinated. When the act takes place, the Doctor finds himself holding the murder weapon. But he is a decoy—the real gunman is the Master. Now at the end of his regeneration cycle, only hatred for the Doctor and his own race keeps the Master alive.

In *The Face of Evil* the TARDIS lands in a jungle where there are the remains of a crashed spaceship. Two civilisations have descended from the original crew—the Tribe of the Sevateem (Survey Team) and over the mountain, the highly advanced religious order, the Tesh (Technicians). Sevateem outcast Leela helps the Doctor investigate the mystery of the great god Xoanon, whose face is carved in the side of the mountain—it is the face of the Doctor himself.

In *The Robots of Death* the Doctor and Leela find themselves on a mining vessel trawling across the desert plains of an alien world. The sandminer is driven by a host of servant robots under the control of a skeleton crew of humans. One of their number has been strangled to death. As the crew are being picked off one by one, the robots are the prime suspects. But who among the human crew has changed the robots' command structure, and why? A great whodunnit in the vein of Agatha Christie.

The Talons of Weng-Chiang sees the TARDIS arriving in nineteenth century London. The Doctor has shed his coat, hat and scarf in favour of a Sherlock Holmes-style cape and dear stalker. Leela is dressed as a lady of the Victorian era. Young women are disappearing and the trail leads to a music hall run by Henry Gordon Jago, and to his latest sensational act Li H'sen Chang and his homicidal mannequin doll Mr Sin. Script writer Robert Holmes combines all the clichés of nineteenth century literature into one great homage–giant rats, mysterious Chinese magicians, killer oriental dolls, and hints of Jack the Ripper. Add to that a time travelling magic cabinet and an ancient Chinese god, and you have a great classic from Seventies *Doctor Who* absolutely dripping with style.

Under Producer Graham Williams (1977-79)

Horror of Fang Rock takes place in a nineteenth century lighthouse. It's another atmospheric whodunnit in a confined area cut off from the outside world. An alien creature called a Rutan has crash-landed in the sea. At the same time a sailing ship has run aground. The Doctor thinks he has successfully locked the Rutan out of the lighthouse, when in fact he's locked it in with them ...

The Stones of Blood is part of the 1978 'Key to Time' season, released in the box set of the same name. The Doctor and Romana have been contracted by the White Guardian to find and assemble the six segments of the legendary Key to Time. They have procured the first two segments (in *The Ribos Operation* and *The Pirate Planet*) and now they've arrived in Cornwall, where strange things are going on at Boscombe Hall. Aided by Professor Rumford, the Doctor uncovers the religious cult of the druid god of war–the Cailleach–and then alien Cessair of Diplos, who is hiding in human guise. This story contained the one hundredth episode of the series and fell on its fifteenth anniversary. It's a great example of the mysterious balanced with the hilarious.

City of Death was originally a script by David Fisher that was then rewritten by script editor (and author of *The Hitchhiker's Guide to the Galaxy*) Douglas Adams over a weekend. On a barren primeval Earth, the alien Scaroth pilots the spaceship carrying what is left of his decimated race. But as the ship lifts off it is caught in a time eddy and is destroyed. Scaroth himself is 'splintered' through time, masquerading as Count Scarlioni in Paris 1979, as Captain Tancredi in Florence 1505, and in ten other guises scattered through history. The Doctor and Romana are on holiday in Paris, 1979, when they find that Scarlioni has somehow come by seven genuine copies of the Mona Lisa and intends to sell them to a secret buyer. But what does he hope to achieve by this? A clever script from Adams is brought to life by a sparkling guest cast (Julian Glover in particular) and complemented by excellent direction, great usage of Paris's tourist attractions and a superb incidental score from Dudley Simpson.

Under Producer John Nathan-Turner (1980-81)

Full Circle is the first adventure in *The E-Space Trilogy* box set and takes place in the 'pocket universe' of E-Space

(Exo Space). The Doctor and Romana expect to find themselves back on Gallifrey–the time-space coordinates are right, but when they step out of the TARDIS they are on the planet Alzarius. The natives are concerned about Mistfall and the creatures that emerge from the swamps at that time, the Marshmen. The planet's inhabitants are encouraged to board the huge starliner and ready for take-off. But not everyone believes in the legend of Mistfall. A band of young rebels refuse to board the ship. They hold Romana hostage and seize the TARDIS. Meanwhile the Doctor confronts the elders who govern the star liner. The three Deciders know more than they're letting on. Mistfall, the Marshmen, the continuous repairs conducted on the spaceship and the evolution of a spider- like species are all connected. One of the rebels, a boy named Adric, senses that he doesn't belong with his people, whether they get on their way or not.

Warriors' Gate is the third instalment of the E-Space trilogy. In an attempt to return to N-Space, the TARDIS has got stuck in a strange white void between the two universes. Another craft is also trapped there, a cargo ship containing lion-like humanoids called Tharils in suspended animation. Tharils are time-sensitive beings that are sold as slaves to different worlds. The Doctor, Romana, Adric and K9 are visited in the TARDIS by an ethereal projection of Biroc, a Tharil. He asks for help to free his people. A derelict church-like structure comes into view. It is a gateway between universes. The Doctor knows he must free the Tharils so they can use the gateway, in spite of the volatile cargo ship captain, and he must do it quickly–because the white void is contracting.

The Keeper of Traken is the penultimate adventure for the Fourth Doctor and is included with *Logopolis* and *Castrovalva* in the *New Beginnings* box set. With Romana and K9 now aiding Biroc in E-Space, the Doctor and Adric have successfully returned to the normal universe. They are visited by an enthroned wizened old man–the Keeper of the Source of the planet Traken, a world united in peace and mutual respect. However, their ideal society has a new arrival, a sentient statue called Melkur, which has planted itself in the grove near the main sanctum. The Keeper will soon die, and he believes that the Melkur is set on seizing the Source for itself during transition to the new Keeper. The Doctor agrees to investigate and is shocked when he discovers what Melkur really is.

Logopolis - The Doctor wants to rid the TARDIS of its police box guise so it will change form and blend in with its surroundings. He sets out to measure a real police box on Earth and then take the measurements to the planet Logopolis, whose inhabitants employ a high form of mathematics to manipulate the relationship between energy and matter–they will use the measurements to reconfigure his TARDIS. As he engages in the task, he witnesses in the distance a shadowy, embryonic figure watching him. Meanwhile, an Australian air hostess named Tegan has broken down on the Barnett Bypass, where the Doctor's ship has materialised around a real police box. Believing it to be the proper police box, she goes inside. Convinced that the Master is on his trail, the Doctor continues on to Logopolis, where he learns its ancient secret. What will the Master do with that knowledge? The Doctor must stop his rival if it's the last thing he does ...

Miscellany

- Outgoing production team Barry Letts and Terrance Dicks had the job of replacing Jon Pertwee as the Doctor. They considered Fulton Mackay and Michael Bentine. The latter would only accept if he could write and direct as well. Letts explained that the filming schedule was so gruelling, there wouldn't be any time to write and direct as well as play the lead. At the same time, actor Tom Baker had written to BBC Head of Series and Serials Bill Slater, asking for employment. He'd starred in theatrical releases *Nicholas and Alexandra* and *The Golden Voyage of Sinbad*, but was currently working as a bricklayer on a building site. Bill Slater introduced Baker to Letts and Dicks, and within minutes they knew they'd found the perfect successor to Jon Pertwee.

- Tom Baker is to date the longest-serving actor to have played the Doctor. He starred in seven seasons from 1974 to 1981. His first story *Robot* was overseen by Barry Letts and Terrance Dicks, before Philip Hinchcliffe became producer and popular *Doctor Who* writer Robert Holmes took up the mantle of script editor. Hinchcliffe desired to raise the series out of its 'children's programme' image and aim it at the intelligent fourteen year old, and Holmes indulged his love of the macabre, creating a number of pastiches of the popular *Hammer Horror* movies. Hinchcliffe's productions were heavily criticised by moral campaigner Mary Whitehouse and overspent on each of his seasons. His successor in 1977, Graham Williams, was told to tone down the violence and stick to the prescribed budget. Robert Holmes was succeeded as script editor in 1978 by Anthony Read, and in 1979 by *Hitchhiker's Guide to the Galaxy* author Douglas Adams. This era is often described as 'cheap and cheerful'. Baker's final season was produced by John Nathan-Turner. Irritated by what he saw as the cheap look of the show and the overindulgence in undergraduate humour, Nathan-Turner commissioned science writer Christopher H Bidmead as his script editor to even out the humour and inject some genuine scientific theory into the proceedings. The series was given a new title sequence, a new arrangement of the theme music, a redesigned outfit for the Doctor, a new police box prop, and Dudley Simpson's six-piece orchestra was dropped in favour of electronic incidental music by composers from the BBC Radiophonic Workshop. Tom Baker didn't care for most aspects of the 'new look' series and offered his resignation.

- Jim Acheson, who would later be an Oscar-winning Hollywood costume designer created the original Fourth Doctor outfit. Acheson was inspired by a Lautrec poster in which a bohemian man wore a long red coat and, a broad-brimmed hat and a scarf. A lady called Begonia Pope was given a lot of different coloured balls of wool and asked to knit the scarf. Begonia interpreted the instructions literally and knitted up all the wool into a ten foot-long scarf. Hinchcliffe was so amused by it that he decided the Doctor should wear it as it was. (In the Graham Williams period, the scarf doubled in length and the Doctor's coat was in a Victorian cut. In his final year, produced by John Nathan-Turner, the whole outfit was given some colour coordination in burgundy and related colours.)

- *Genesis of the Daleks* was actually commissioned by Barry Letts and Terrance Dicks, who rejected a script from Terry Nation that was almost identical to his previous one. Letts suggested that Nation pen a story showing how the Daleks were created. To give a more human-sounding spokesman for the Daleks, Nation invented their creator Davros. The character was such a success that the writer insisted he be included in all Dalek stories from then on. *Genesis* is frequently voted in fan polls as the best *Doctor Who* adventure ever.

- In *Revenge of the Cybermen*, we learn that the metal giants are weakened by exposure to gold.

- The original police box prop, created by Peter Brachacki and featured throughout the series since its first episode in 1963, had been bolstered and redressed numerous times. During William Hartnell's era it had white window frames, a St John's Ambulance badge on the right-hand door (like a real police box) and no door handles. Then, in Patrick Troughton's reign, the window frames were painted the same colour as the box, the ambulance badge disappeared and the right-hand door acquired a handle. The prop had a number of different roofs and lamps in its time, but by the time it reached Tom Baker's second season it had seen better days. Legend has it that when in *The Seeds of Doom*, Baker and Elisabeth Sladen went inside and shut the door, the roof fell in on them! Hinchcliffe assigned Barry Newbery to create a new lightweight prop that would be easier to assemble on location. It had a flat roof and no door handles, but only lasted three years. John Nathan-Turner wanted a box that looked more like the real thing. In 1980, viewers were blessed with a prop that had a stacked roof, a door handle, and a little handle on the panel that housed the telephone. In Baker's final story *Logopolis*, we saw for the first time a police officer making a call from such a box.

• In Hinchcliffe's final season (1976-77), the Doctor in *The Masque of Mandragora* walks the maze of TARDIS corridors and stumbles across the secondary control room. The walls are wood-panelled, and the 'roundels' are in stained glass. The central console is sans the glass column that rises and falls and looks more like a bureau, while the controls are hidden beneath wooden flaps. This Jules Verne-inspired design lasted no more than one season, as the wood-panelled walls warped in storage. In the second story of Graham Williams' first season, *The Invisible Enemy*, the TARDIS returned to a design closer to the original concept.

• Sarah Jane Smith leaves the Doctor at the end of *The Hand of Fear*. Baker and Sladen were permitted to embellish the script and improvise a genuinely moving parting of the ways. Sarah was so popular with viewers, Nathan-Turner hoped she would guest star in Tom Baker's final story to smooth over the regeneration into his successor (to, in effect, 'hold the hand' of younger viewers who would miss Baker), but she declined. She did, however, reprise the role in 1981 for the pilot of ill-fated spin-off series *K9 and Company*, and starred opposite Jon Pertwee in twentieth anniversary special *The Five Doctors*. In 2006, she returned to guest star opposite David Tennant before taking the lead in Children's BBC's hugely successful spin-off *The Sarah Jane Adventures*.

- In *The Deadly Assassin*, the TARDIS is referred to as a Type Forty model.

- K9 was devised by Bob Baker and Dave Martin for their script *The Invisible Enemy*. It was only intended to appear in that story as Professor Marius' mobile computer and was going to be like a robot Doberman with an actor inside. But designer Tony Harding chose to realise it as a small radio-controlled prop. Actor John Leeson was hired to provide a squeaky voice for the character. Recognising that it would be a possible hit with the children, two endings were filmed–one where the Doctor and Leela bid Marius and K9 farewell, and one where Marius offers the dog to the Doctor. In the season climax *The Invasion of Time*, K9 remains with Leela on Gallifrey and the Doctor brings out of storage K9 MKII, which he's built himself. John Leeson voiced the character for two seasons, followed by David Brierley in the third. The prop itself was a pain to work with, taking up valuable filming time with its malfunctions. When John Nathan-Turner became producer, he vowed to get rid of the character (because of the mechanical problems and because writers used it too often to get the Doctor out of sticky situations). John Leeson was hired to provide the voice again until K9 was written out. Christmas 1981 saw a pilot episode for *K9 and Company* in which Sarah Jane Smith receives K9 MKIII, a gift from the Doctor. A full series did not materialise. Sarah and K9 returned in *The Five Doctors* (1983) and *School Reunion* (2006). In the latter he was destroyed while battling the Krillitanes. The Doctor built K9 MKIV for Sarah. K9 made regular appearances in *The Sarah Jane Adventures*. The character's co-creator Dave Martin produced a series for the Ten Network, Australia, in which the original prop is reborn as a small CGI version and aids a group of youths to fight crime. Titled *K-9*, it ran for one season. In all these instances, K9 was voiced by John Leeson.

- 1979's opening story *Destiny of the Daleks* played host to the very first female regeneration, as Time Lady Romana, played by Mary Tamm the previous year, was now played by Lalla Ward (who had been Lady Astra in the previous season finale). The new Romana walks in and the Doctor tells her she can't have Princess Astra's form, so she comes from her quarters several times with different incarnations before finally settling on Princess Astra again. Members of the *Doctor Who* Appreciation Society were not impressed by the way Romana put on different bodies the way a woman might choose a dress. No physical transformation from Mary Tamm to Lalla Ward was shown on screen. Fans saw the jokey set piece as a massive wasted opportunity.

- The final story of the seventeenth season (1979) was to have been *Shada* by Douglas Adams. All the location filming was completed, but because of union strikes the studio recordings were abandoned. The incomplete adventure was never broadcast. The scene where the Doctor and Romana punt down the River Cam in Cambridge was used to represent the Fourth Doctor in the twentieth anniversary special *The Five Doctors*, as Tom Baker had declined to appear in the celebratory episode. In 1992 all the existing material of *Shada* itself was released with linking narration performed by Baker straight to home video.

- Following the death of actor Roger Delgado in 1973, it would be three years until the character of the Master returned. Writer Robert Holmes devised the plot device whereby a Time Lord can only regenerate twelve times. After his thirteenth life is spent, he must face death. When the Master returned in *The Deadly Assassin*, he was played by Peter Pratt, and later in *The Keeper of Traken* by Geoffrey Beevers, as a barely living emaciated corpse desperate to extend his life. In Tom Baker's final season, Anthony Ainley was cast as the restored Master.

- The series' theme music was composed by Ron Grainer and arranged by Delia Derbyshire of the BBC Radiophonic Workshop in 1963. The ethereal arrangement was made by recording individual notes from an oscilloscope, as well as playing glass tubes and an organ, and synchronising the sounds on spools of tape. Delia added extra sounds in the late Sixties, and then in the Seventies included the famous 'electronic scream' as a sting to herald the closing music. But in 1980, producer John Nathan-Turner commissioned Peter Howell of the BBC Radiophonic Workshop to produce a completely new realisation of the tune using the then state of the art Fairlight synthesiser. Tom Baker favoured Delia's 1970s arrangement and the change was one of many that compelled him to move on. Howell's version of the theme served the series up to and including the 1985 season.

- Graphic designer Bernard Lodge created all the title sequences from 1963's time winds/howl-around effect, to 1967's sequence featuring the Doctor's face and 1970's full colour version. In 1974 he made the most famous titles animation, employing a technique called slit-scan. In this the TARDIS slid up a 'time corridor' before opening out into a 'time vortex'. The Doctor's face came through the mist before Lodge's diamond-shaped logo glided down into oblivion. The blue and white shapes in the vortex were apparently taken from Tesco shopping bags! However, in 1980, Bernard Lodge's sequence was dispensed with. John Nathan-Turner wanted a completely new design to go with Peter Howell's theme music. He approached designer Sid Sutton to create a moving star field that forms the Doctor's face and new 'neon' tube-lettered logo. Variations of this sequence served the series up to and including the 1986 season.

- Shortly after leaving *Doctor Who*, actress Lalla Ward married Tom Baker. Sadly, the marriage only lasted for a couple of years.

- The success of the Tom Baker era cannot be understated. Throughout the six of his seven years in the role, most stories averaged around ten to twelve million viewers. In 1979, viewing figures peaked at sixteen million thanks to ITV experiencing industrial action and there only being two other channels to choose from. To date, *City of Death* is the most watched *Doctor Who* adventure ever. But, just as John Nathan-Turner was launching the new look 1980 season, ITV unveiled their competition in the form of the lavish American-produced *Buck Rogers in the 25th Century*. With its glamorous stars Gil Gerard and Erin Gray, cute robot Twiki (voiced by Mel Blanc) and impressive special effects, it trounced *Doctor Who* in the ratings. Tom Baker's finale was watched by six million people in March 1981.

CHAPTER 5

THE DOCTOR
As played by
Peter Davison

1982-84

The Fifth Doctor is younger in appearance and more dynamic than the fourth incarnation. This Doctor dresses like an Edwardian cricketer with a Panama hat, beige coat, stripy trousers and V-neck jumper, although despite his love of the sport we only see him play cricket once during his tenure. His costume is completed by a stick of celery on his lapel, the meaning of which we only discover in his very last story.

We see a more human side to this Doctor and he is less prone to some of the eccentric excesses of his predecessors, although he does have a tendency towards flippancy, often bringing him into conflict with those in authority. His human qualities are highlighted when he confronts the emotionless Cybermen and asks if they have ever smelt a flower or watched a beautiful sunset, things which mean so much to us but that are meaningless to them. We see the extent of the Fifth Doctor's morality when he is given the chance to destroy the evil Davros but hesitates and is unable to do so.

This Doctor cares deeply for his companions, and although there are frictions between him and those he travels with, the deep affections they all have for each other become evident over time. When one of those companions tragically perishes, we realise that the Doctor is by no means invincible and that his ability to control events will only stretch so far. This is also illustrated by his failure to create peace between humans and Silurians, a race for whom he has had a long-standing respect.

Who is the Doctor?

The Doctor's fourth regeneration does not pass as smoothly as his previous changes, and his new incarnation needs to recuperate in a previously unseen part of the TARDIS known as the Zero Room. As he recovers, the TARDIS is drawn towards Event One, the massive hydrogen inrush which occurred at the beginning of the universe, and he is forced to jettison twenty-five percent of the time machine in order to prevent it from being destroyed.

Appearing to be a man in his early thirties and with none of the gravitas of his previous selves, the Doctor lulls his adversaries into a false sense of security. They have no idea that they're dealing with an alien who is hundreds of years old.

There are disagreements between the Doctor and his companions, particularly with Adric and Tegan, but the Doctor's sadness and frustration are all too evident when Adric dies following an encounter with the Cybermen. The Doctor loses another old 'friend' when, during an encounter with a race of aliens called the Terileptils in the time of the Black Death, his beloved sonic screwdriver is destroyed.

The Doctor once again comes into conflict with his own people, the Time Lords, and is sentenced to death, but manages to escape this fate when the situation transpires to have been manipulated by his old enemy Omega, aided by a corrupt Time Lord called Hedin, previously a friend of the Doctor's.

Later, the alien Mawdryn attempts to steal the Doctor's remaining regenerations, but aided by the Brigadier the Doctor defeats him.

The Doctor encounters his previous incarnations when an unknown force reactivates the ancient Game of Rassilon in the Death Zone on Gallifrey. The Doctors outwit their adversary and are all returned to their own time streams. As a reward, the Time Lords make him Lord President of Gallifrey, a position he abdicates immediately. Sometime after this, the Doctor prevents an attempt by the Daleks to assassinate the High Council of the Time Lords.

In his final adventure, the Fifth Doctor reveals that the reason for the celery on his lapel (which he has worn since his first story) is that it detects certain gases in the Praxis range, to which he is allergic.

It is fitting that this most human of Doctors dies not saving the universe or even a planet, but giving his life simply to save a friend. Following an incident on the planet Androzani Minor, both the Doctor and his companion Peri are riddled with poison and there is only enough of the antidote for one of them. The Doctor makes the ultimate sacrifice, and so the change begins again ...

Try these on DVD!

In *Kinda*, while Nyssa is recuperating in the TARDIS, the Doctor, Tegan and Adric explore the paradise world of Deva Loka. The world is home to the mysterious Kinda, a race of mute telepaths who resent the presence of a human scientific settlement. When Tegan falls asleep beneath some mystical chimes, an ancient evil force called the Mara enters her mind. Using Tegan as a host, the Mara is intent on destroying the Kinda. A highly original adventure, some of its concepts have their roots in Buddhism. (Available with its sequel, *Snakedance*, in the *Mara Tales* box set.)

The Visitation is a good straightforward and traditional adventure for the Doctor. The Time Lord and his companions try to return Tegan to Heathrow Airport, but arrive instead during the time of the Black Death where the Grim Reaper is, quite literally, stalking the countryside. The Doctor meets a new reptilian adversary in the form of the Terileptils and discovers how the Great Fire of London really started ...

Earthshock - The Doctor, Nyssa, Tegan and Adric find themselves in a cave in Earth's future. Looking at fossils of dinosaurs, the Doctor ponders what happened to cause the extinction of the mighty reptiles. The time travellers bump into a military team led by Lieutenant Scott and are accused of murdering a missing geologist. Two sinister black androids appear to be guarding something in the cave–what is it and who is controlling them? The Doctor discovers that the Cybermen have returned and are planning to blow up an important interstellar alliance conference. Will they succeed, and how does this all tie in with the ultimate fate of the dinosaurs?

In *Mawdryn Undead* the TARDIS is on a collision course with a spaceship that is linked to a public school in both 1977 and 1983. In 1983 a transmat booth is discovered by one of the pupils, a boy named Turlough, who is really an exiled alien. He is transported to the ship, where he meets the Doctor. An old adversary of the Doctor's called the Black Guardian makes a deal with the boy–kill the Time Lord, and then he will be helped to escape Earth. When Tegan uses the booth to follow the Doctor to Earth, it materialises in 1977. There she finds Brigadier Lethbridge-Stewart, who has retired from UNIT and is now teaching A-level mathematics. In 1983, the Doctor also meets the Brigadier. Even after explaining that he has regenerated since their last adventure together, the Brigadier has no idea who the Doctor is. Words like 'TARDIS' mean nothing to him. Why has the Brigadier lost his memory? Who is Turlough, really? And how does the ailing Mawdryn plan to restore himself? (This story is the first adventure of *The Black Guardian Trilogy* box set).

Enlightenment - a prize much sought after by the Eternals, ethereal beings who take on human form. The TARDIS materialises in the hold of a nineteenth century sailing ship. The crew are very strange–they don't seem to remember where they set sail from. Crewman Marriner seems particularly interested in Tegan, which unnerves her. Captain Striker is decidedly uncooperative when quizzed by the Doctor. What is going on? The ship is engaged in a race. Then the Doctor goes up top. The crewmen are Eternals and the fleet of sailing ships are in space! Can Turlough be trusted, and how does the evil Black Guardian plan to manipulate him and the race to destroy the Doctor? (Another high-concept story, this is the final adventure in *The Black Guardian Trilogy*. It may be watched as originally broadcast or with enhanced CGI effects.)

In *The Five Doctors*, the first five incarnations of the Doctor are taken out of time and placed in the Death Zone on Gallifrey, where they are forced to recreate the ancient Game of Rassilon. Aided by former companions such as Susan, the Brigadier and Sarah Jane Smith, they must avoid old adversaries, including the Cybermen and Yeti, and try to get to the Dark Tower. But what unseen force has brought them there, and what are his intentions?

The Awakening - An ancient evil lies dormant in a church in the quintessentially English village of Little Hodcombe. Sir George Hutchinson is hoping to recreate the English Civil War down to the last detail. But is he taking things a little too far? Can the legendary Malus really harness the negative energy generated by the war games to free itself? Time is affected, and a boy from the village in the seventeenth century crosses into the present day. The Doctor must stop the war games and prevent the awakening. This creepy two-part adventure has a sparkling script, a great cast, good use of location filming and atmospheric incidental music. It is an underrated gem.

Resurrection of the Daleks - With Davros, Daleks and ray guns being fired left, right and centre, this is good science fiction which takes a more poignant turn when Tegan decides it's time to take her leave from the Doctor ...

The Caves of Androzani is believed by many fans to be the greatest *Doctor Who* story ever made and it's not hard to see why. There is certainly little to rival its script and direction. There is the serious subject matter of drug running and a superior villain in the form of Sharaz Jek, brilliantly underplayed by Christopher Gable. Even a rather dodgy monster called the Magma beast can't spoil the overall quality of this one. The Fifth Doctor's swansong is action-adventure, a political satire, it has a gritty tone to it, and there is some darkly comic dialogue. It is Peter Davison's finest ninety minutes. A must see!

Miscellany

- Producer John Nathan-Turner had approached actor Richard Griffiths to star as the Fifth Doctor but ultimately opted for Peter Davison after looking at a photograph of him at a charity cricket match. The two men had worked together on the successful BBC One drama *All Creatures Great and Small*. The youthful, fair-haired Davison was intended to be a marked contrast to the more mature, curly-haired Tom Baker. At the age of twenty-nine, Davison was the youngest actor up until that point to be cast in the role.

- Aware that younger audiences might only be familiar with Tom Baker's Doctor after the actor's record-breaking seven years in the role, John Nathan-Turner arranged for a series of repeats of the old Doctors' stories to be shown on BBC Two prior to transmission of Davison's first season. *The Five Faces of Doctor Who* comprised the following stories: *An Unearthly Child* with William Hartnell, *The Krotons* with Patrick Troughton, *Carnival of Monsters* and *The Three Doctors* with Jon Pertwee and *Logopolis* with Tom Baker, climaxing with just a glimpse of Peter Davison.

- For the first time, *Doctor Who* was shown during the week rather than on a Saturday–twice a week on Monday/Tuesday for Davison's first season, Tuesday/Wednesday for his second and Thursday/Friday for his third.

- John Nathan-Turner was a skilled publicist and never missed an opportunity to promote *Doctor Who* in the press. As well as signing up star names for the Davison era such as Stratford Johns, Beryl Reid and British movie actor Richard Todd, he was able to acquire the use of British Airways' Concorde plane for the story *Time-Flight*. He also utilised foreign locations so that the Fifth Doctor and team travelled to both Amsterdam and Lanzarote.

- When shown an animatronic mannequin by its creator Mike Power, John Nathan-Turner was so excited that he had it written into *Doctor Who* as a companion. Named Kamelion in the series, the robot has the ability to change into various humanoid guises. In its debut story *The King's Demons*, Kamelion is masquerading as King John in 1215 AD, just prior to his signing Magna Carta. The robot isn't seen again (or even referred to) until its second and final appearance a year later in *Planet of Fire*. In this, the Master gains control of it. With regret, the Doctor has no option but to destroy it. On both of its appearances, Kamelion was voiced by actor Gerald Flood.

- Future Doctor Colin Baker makes his first *Doctor Who* appearance in the Season 20 opener *Arc of Infinity*, in which he plays Commander Maxil of the Gallifreyan Chancellery Guard and actually shoots the Doctor! He was the only actor to be cast as the Doctor having previously had a role in the series– until Peter Capaldi in 2013.

- The story *Mawdryn Undead* was originally supposed to feature the return of Ian Chesterton, the teacher befriended by the First Doctor during his early adventures. When actor William Russell proved unavailable, Nicholas Courtney was asked to reprise the role of Brigadier Lethbridge-Stewart instead. Hence the Brigadier is shown, rather curiously, teaching maths in a boys' school. The story is a continuity oddity in that the Brigadier is suggested to have retired from UNIT in the 1970s, whereas it had been previously hinted that his UNIT adventures were possibly set during the 1980s.

- Look out for actor Martin Clunes, later to star in sit-com, *Men Behaving Badly* and ITV drama *Doc Martin*, appearing in his first television role as Prince Lon in *Snakedance*. Other guest stars later to achieve fame include *EastEnders* regular Leslie Grantham in *Resurrection of the Daleks* and Robert Glenister in *The Caves of Androzani*.

- By the time the twentieth anniversary story *The Five Doctors* was made, William Hartnell had sadly passed away, so the role of the First Doctor was played by actor Richard Hurndall. Tom Baker refused to return, feeling that he had only recently left the series and did not want to appear alongside other Doctors, so he was represented by footage from *Shada*, a Fourth Doctor story that was never completed due to a strike at the BBC. Unlike most *Doctor Who* stories, this adventure was first broadcast as one ninety minute special rather than four twenty-five minute episodes. The anniversary was also marked by a huge convention at Longleat House in Wiltshire. The success of the event surprised the BBC, and the surrounding roads were jammed with traffic as thousands of fans struggled to get to the event.

- Production of *Warriors of the Deep* was marred by the loss of by two weeks of studio time, due to Mrs Thatcher calling the 1983 general election. With less time available, shortcuts had to be made and the Myrka costume was still wet with green paint when filming began. Consequently, green paint can sometimes be seen on the set and the actors!

- Due to the 1984 Olympics, *Resurrection of the Daleks* was broadcast as two forty-five minute episodes instead of four twenty-five minute instalments. This format would be adopted by the programme when Colin Baker began his first full season the following year.

CHAPTER 6

THE DOCTOR
As played by
Colin Baker

1984-86

If the Fifth Doctor was the reserved but stalwart 'English' gentleman, the Sixth is a manic barometer. The moment he sits up, he is very much present. His eyes are keen and sharp. When a confused Peri wonders how he can be the same man, he responds with a sarcastic quip. It has been a timely change, he thinks, and not a moment too soon.

The Doctor is very pleased with his new self and admires his appearance in a mirror. He then chooses an outfit, bragging about his impeccable sartorial taste—red shoes with green spats, yellow and black 'humbug' trousers, a knitted waistcoat (with green pocket watch), a green cravat with white spots and a multicoloured patchwork coat.

The regeneration process has produced an instability, ranging from moments of manic violence (he tries to kill Peri) to whimpering cowardice. He gradually settles, but reminds his companion that he is an alien and by definition will have different customs and values. Whatever she makes of them, he is the Doctor—whether she likes it or not.

Together they battle Cybermen who are trying to stop the events of 1966's *The Tenth Planet* coming true—their home world is destroyed. They encounter the slimiest businessman ever in the form of the slug-like Sil, have dealings with the Master and the Rani in the Industrial Revolution, and meet one of the Doctor's other selves in twentieth century Spain. Add to that a despotic mutant ruling a small isolated citadel on the planet Karfel and Davros raiding graves on Necros to build a new generation of subservient Daleks, and the twenty-second season is a success.

When we next meet the pair, the Doctor has mellowed a little and Peri has matured. And then she's gone. The

Doctor finds himself taken out of time and placed on a Time Lord space station where he must stand trial for breaking the cardinal rule of Gallifrey, that of meddling in the affairs of other peoples and, to their detriment, affecting cultural developments. This seems trivial to the Doctor, as he's already faced trial for those 'crimes', and following his exile has been pretty much left to his own devices. But as the trial reaches the events of his most recent adventure, the odds are suddenly stacked against him. After a shock revelation, the Doctor must present an episode from his near future to show that his behaviour improves– but scenes have been subtly altered to cast him in a bad light. The Time Lords seem determined to have him executed–but what staggering truth are they hiding?

Who is the Doctor?

With his theatrical outfit, bombastic outbursts and obscure literary quotes, the Sixth Doctor is a man of learning and a moral crusader. He's a man of extremes, filled with joy at meeting an old Time Lord mentor on Jaconda, but so enraged by Mestor's diabolical scheme to scatter gastropod eggs across the galaxy that he risks a brain embolism to stop him.

Alien and detached, the Doctor often fails to empathise with Peri. He cannot understand why she's so afraid when he pilots the TARDIS dangerously close to Halley's Comet. He thinks it's amusing to mimic her American accent and correct her grammar. Yet he has deep affection for her and will put his life on the line to save her. When he thinks the Time Lords have massacred a whole research station to protect the secret of time travel he is indignant, but when he believes the universe may collapse in just a few centuries he soliloquises about the beauty of sunsets and frailty of butterflies.

The Doctor, as do all Time Lords, shares a symbiotic link with his TARDIS. He is now over 900 hundred years old. He finds fishing restful but loathes carrot juice. He can barely rise out of his chair when called to respect the Inquisitor as she takes her seat for his trial. The Doctor goes on record declaring that his own race is decadent, degenerate and rotten to the core. Ten millions years of absolute power has made them totally corrupt.

The court is depending on the volatile Doctor's appetite for melodrama and romanticism–if they give him enough rope he will hang himself, and the prosecuting counsellor knows which buttons to press. In fact, he knows the Doctor better than anyone else ever could ...

Try These on DVD!

Attack of the Cybermen - Interplanetary mercenary Lytton (last seen in the previous year's *Resurrection of the Daleks*) is now masquerading as a powerful crime boss. With a small band of thugs he enters London's sewers to raid a high street bank–or that's what he tells them. In reality he is endeavouring to contact the Cybermen, who have a base in the sewers. They and their counterparts on their adopted planet Telos know that their home world was destroyed in 1986. Using a time vessel, they intend to prevent the attack from Earth and change history. With the aid of Telos' original inhabitants, the Cryons, the Doctor sets out to thwart the Cyber plan. But has he misjudged Lytton? This story has lots of continuity references but is a great example of a multilayered plot where you don't understand everything that is going on until the end.

In *Vengeance on Varos* the Doctor and Peri find themselves in the Punishment Dome on the planet Varos. There they meet a young rebel named Jondar, who is chained to the wall with a laser cannon trained on him. He must anticipate when the laser will fire and try to avoid disintegration. The torture is being broadcast as entertainment. When business rep Sil comes to negotiate fees for Varos' precious minerals, he is enthralled by the tapes. But revolution is brewing on that barren world ... This is a great parody of the issue of violence on television and the way people can be influenced and controlled by what they watch. It also boasts one of the best villains in the series.

The Mark of the Rani sees the TARDIS materialise in the north of England during the Industrial Revolution. An exiled Time Lord chemist called the Rani has set her base amidst the Luddite revolt so she can remain undetected and draw from the Luddites' brains the chemical that induces sleep. But the Master is also present and wishes to unleash a trap that will humiliate the Doctor. Perceiving the Doctor to be a scientist and inventor, the Luddites seize our hero. The Rani is completely amoral. To her, the side effects of her experimentation on inferior species (in this case nineteenth century humans) are irrelevant. All she cares about is achieving her goal.

The Two Doctors has, by pure chance, the current Doctor crossing paths with his second incarnation and his companion Jamie McCrimmon. In a clever and witty script from Robert Holmes, the Doctor and Peri visit a space station to see Dastari, an eminent scientist–only to find that everyone has been massacred and Dastari is gone. The station computer reports that the Time Lords did it. The Doctor mind-links with his former self, who had been on board the station with Jamie just prior to the attack, and discovers he is being held prisoner in Seville, Spain. A primitive alien woman called Chessene has been augmented by Dastari to genius level and is now bent on learning the secret of time travel from the Second Doctor. She has enlisted the help of two Sontarans, promising them usage of her time machine once the vital element has been procured from the Doctor's brain–the symbiotic nuclei that links him telepathically to the TARDIS.

Revelation of the Daleks - The Doctor and Peri arrive on Necros, home to Tranquil Repose, a place where those who are dying from terminal illnesses may have their bodies cryogenically frozen until a cure can be found. For an extra fee they can have a disc jockey deliver the latest galactic news and their favourite Earth pop music directly into their unconscious minds. The Doctor goes to pay his respects to a renowned scientist, but instead finds a statue of himself in the Garden of Fond Memories–someone has lured him to the planet. Davros is masquerading as 'the Great Healer' and using brain tissue from those in the catacombs to create a new generation of Daleks that can reproduce themselves automatically. While the Daleks are in this story, it is really Davros's show. Actor Terry Molly relishes the part, and Eric Saward's script is laced with black humour.

The Trial of a Time Lord is really four stories linked by the 'umbrella' theme of the Doctor being tried by his own people. It formed the whole of the twenty-third season.

The first four parts deal with the Doctor and Peri's adventure on Ravolox, a planet in the Stellian galaxy. The planet has the same atmosphere composition and angle of tilt to Earth. Then Peri discovers the remains of an underground railway station called Marble Arch! How has Earth been moved two light years from its original position, and why?

The second four-part story is the one in which the Doctor was involved when he was taken out of time to stand trial. He and Peri are investigating sales of a sophisticated deadly weapon to a primitive culture of warriors. They are on Thoros Beta, which is the home to Sil and the Mentors. Sil's superior, Lord Kiv, needs his brain transplanted into another body to escape a degenerative illness. But scientist Crozier wants to go beyond that–he wants to achieve mind transference. The Doctor is put in the machine and has his mind scrambled. As a result he becomes decidedly self-serving and horrible to Peri. Watching these events from the court room, the Doctor cannot remember some of the sequences and accuses the prosecution of editing the evidence. But then comes the real shock: Crozier has found the perfect body for Kiv's mind transference ...

Stunned by the climax to the events on Thoros Beta, the Doctor presents evidence from his near future in the third four-part adventure. The Doctor and new companion Melanie respond to a distress call and materialise in the cargo hold of a space liner. Scientists are transporting giant vegetation pods. When the pods burst open, the crew and passengers on the liner begin to disappear. Plant creatures called Vervoids regard animal kind as their enemy. Who among the humans is also guilty of murder? The Doctor must take drastic measures to stop the Vervoids, measures that bring a new charge in the court room—genocide.

In the final two episodes of the trial, the Doctor uncovers the mystery surrounding Earth's relocation and new identity. The truth will rock Time Lord society to its foundations. That sanctimonious band of hypocrites have been covering their tracks. But the Doctor's personal world is shaken further when he discovers what lengths his own people will go to to silence him and who the court prosecutor really is ...

Miscellany

• Having already appeared in the Fifth Doctor story *Arc of Infinity*, Colin Baker was invited to a wedding, where producer John Nathan-Turner saw him entertaining the guests. Baker's larger-than-life persona seemed the perfect contrast to that of Peter Davison, and Nathan-Turner remembered this when it was time to cast Davison's successor. Thrilled to be offered the role, Colin Baker met up with the producer and his script editor Eric Saward to discuss how he would like to play the part. Baker wanted to make him more like William Hartnell's interpretation, moody and unpredictable. He was also keen to highlight the alien nature of the Doctor, stating that he would be the kind of person who could stroll across a pile of dead bodies unconcerned, and then cry because a butterfly has perished.

- When asked how he would like to be dressed as the Doctor, Baker said he wanted to wear black, as sleuths do not draw attention to themselves by wearing outlandish costumes. But John Nathan-Turner dismissed this in favour of the idea that the Sixth Doctor had appalling dress sense. Pat Godfrey came up with several designs, none of which were deemed bad enough. Legend has it that she quickly scribbled a design on her pad and the producer excitedly said yes. In recent times, Baker has stated that the costume sent out the wrong message about the character to the viewer.

- The Sixth Doctor's debut, *The Twin Dilemma*, was broadcast at the end of Peter Davison's final season. The producer worried that nine months was too long a gap between the regeneration and Baker's first full appearance.

- In 1985, the programme was returned to its traditional Saturday teatime slot, but for the first time in twenty-two years, the serials were broadcast as two episodes of forty-five minutes each rather than four times twenty-one and a half minutes.

- *Attack of the Cybermen* saw the TARDIS' chameleon circuit temporarily repaired so that it changed from a police box into a tasteless piece of furniture, then into an organ, then a pair of gates, before finally getting stuck as a police box again. John Nathan-Turner had caused controversy among fans and the tabloid press by stating that he planned to get rid of the police box exterior because police boxes were no longer common on Britain's streets. It has been said since that this was merely a publicity stunt. But given the radical changes the producer made to other icons of the series, like the theme music, title sequence, and sonic screwdriver, it does make one wonder if he would have 'updated' the TARDIS had he felt that he could get away with it.

- Continuing the celebratory tone of the previous year, the series heavily referenced its own past and mythology. It was feared by some fans that this self-indulgent approach may potentially alienate 'casual' viewers, who would struggle to follow the narrative when they dipped in and out of the programme. That said, the season retained the viewing figures of the previous year and was watched by an average audience of seven million.

- Under pressure from accountants who had been brought into the BBC to solve its financial crisis, BBC One controller Michael Grade examined all the expensive programmes in production. He cancelled a number of long-running series, such as the zoo drama *One By One*. Having nothing but disdain for science fiction, he and Head of Series and Serials Jonathan Powell wasted no time in cancelling the third and final series of John Christopher's *Tripods* trilogy. Grade was already on record as stating he could never understand why the BBC insisted on producing *Doctor Who*, as it was such an embarrassment to the Corporation, so it was unsurprising that he would try to cancel that too. However, fans within the BBC got wind of the news and leaked it to the tabloid press.

Michael Grade said he wasn't cancelling the series but was resting it for eighteen months. To justify the decision, he criticised the programme for being too violent and lacking humour. During the hiatus, no notes were given to Nathan-Turner and Saward as to how *Doctor Who* might be improved.

- Upon the series' return, Eric Saward approached popular scribe Robert Holmes to help him shape Season 23. They chose to reflect the trial of the television programme in the narrative of the story, with the Doctor facing trial by his own people. Holmes took inspiration from Charles Dickens' *A Christmas Carol*, and suggested making the first story about the Doctor's recent past, the middle story about the Doctor's present and the third instalment about his future. The trial would climax with the Doctor and his adversary plummeting into oblivion like Sherlock Holmes and Moriarty in Arthur Conan Doyle's *The Final Problem*.

- When Nicola Bryant's character Peri bowed out, the producer hired light entertainment star Bonnie Langford to play new companion Melanie Bush, a computer programmer from Pease Pottage. Writers of *Doctor Who* fanzines were extremely critical of the casting. Her first appearance is in the Doctor's future encounter with the Vervoids, where she is already established as travelling with him. The Doctor, watching the events on a screen in the courtroom, meets her for the first time in the penultimate episode of the season. Mel's first encounter with him (from her perspective) is never revealed. Yes, it's complicated!

- Robert Holmes was contracted to write the first four-part serial, set on Ravolox, with the Thoros Beta segment by Philip Martin, and the Vervoid story by Pip & Jane Baker. Robert Holmes would pen the final two episodes. Part way through writing the penultimate instalment, Holmes suffered a brief illness and passed away. Deeply affected, script editor Eric Saward completed the final two episodes based on Holmes' notes. However, John Nathan-Turner rejected the ending, feeling that it would invite cancellation, there being a question mark over the Doctor's survival. Irritated by JN-T's meddling and general approach to the programme, Saward resigned and left Nathan-Turner to edit the remaining scripts himself. With a lawyer present (to make sure none of Saward's ideas were used), the producer gave a set of location photographs to Pip and Jane Baker and the story so far so they could write the ending he desired.

- Completely disillusioned with the show, Eric Saward granted an interview to *Starburst* magazine in which he accused John Nathan-Turner of pandering to the small cult of fans in America rather than concentrating on good writing. He also said that Colin Baker lacked star quality and should never have been cast as the Doctor.

- In order to give the new series a fresh feel, Nathan-Turner dropped the BBC Radiophonic Workshop and hired freelance composers. The Workshop musicians welcomed this move, as they were feeling overworked. A young composer named Dominic Glynn had sent tape recordings of original music to the producer. As a result he was commissioned to write the score for the first segment of the trial as well as the last two episodes. Impressed by his work, the producer asked if he could realise a new interpretation of the theme music as well. Glynn had nine days to complete the piece.

- Season 23 was broadcast as fourteen twenty-five minute episodes in the autumn of 1986.

- Viewing figures for *The Trial of a Time Lord* peaked at 4.9 million, a significant drop from the previous season. The serial was broadcast opposite two immensely popular ITV shows, *Robin of Sherwood* and the America-imported *The A-Team*. Rather than consider his own scheduling or his decision to rest *Doctor Who* for eighteen months, Michael Grade laid the blame for the programme's failure at Colin Baker's door. He instructed John Nathan-Turner to recast the part of the Doctor.

CHAPTER 7

THE DOCTOR
As played by
Sylvester McCoy

1987-89 and 1996

If the Sixth Doctor was loud and bombastic, the Seventh is quieter, more reflective and more mysterious. At first, the seventh incarnation seems to revel in tomfoolery and inaccurately quotes common proverbs to great comic effect. But he is also capable of immense sensitivity, reassuring his companion Mel that he is still the same man, or comforting the young Welsh girl Ray when her beloved partner finds love elsewhere.

The Seventh Doctor ditches his predecessor's multicoloured coat in favour of a question-mark pullover, Panama hat, cream jacket and battered brolly. As time progresses, the Doctor becomes darker and more brooding, and he adopts a brown coat to reflect this.

This Doctor is arguably the most manipulative of the Time Lord's incarnations and he appears to be playing chess on an intergalactic scale, setting up one situation in order to cause another to happen, with some of his plans taking centuries to play out. Despite this, he always retains his sense of decency and justice, and in quieter moments proves to be thoughtful and philosophical. He shares the other Doctors' sense of adventure and builds up a strong rapport with his companion Ace, taking it upon himself to educate her about the universe and help her face her fears. Quirky and anti-establishment, the Seventh Doctor is nonetheless prepared to work with the military, including his old friend the Brigadier, in order to help the planet Earth resist alien invasion.

Who is the Doctor?

Shortly after his regeneration the Seventh Doctor reveals that he is nine hundred and fifty-three years old, the same age as his arch nemesis Time Lady the Rani, with whom he studied on Gallifrey and whom he faces in his first adventure in his new persona. During his battle with the Daleks in Shoreditch, London in 1963, he drops hints to Ace that he may in fact be much older than this and could have been a contemporary of the Gallifreyans Rassilon and Omega, who originally developed time travel. Confronting Davros, the Doctor claims to be President Elect of the High Council of Time Lords, although he has in fact long since been deposed from this role. To Davros' horror, the Doctor tricks him into using the Hand of Omega, an ancient weapon which he acquired in his first incarnation, to destroy Skaro.

The Doctor later meets Lady Peinforte, who has travelled from the seventeenth century to 1988 in search of the Nemesis statue. Lady Peinforte claims to have information about the Doctor from Gallifrey's Time of Chaos, but when she threatens to reveal these dark mysteries to the Cyber-Leader, the cyborg states that he has no interest in Time Lord secrets.

The Doctor seems to have been somewhat forgotten by UNIT personnel when he encounters the organisation again after the Brigadier's retirement, possibly in the 1990s. It would also appear that in another dimension, a future Doctor may be Merlin from the Arthurian legends. It is apparent he has previously encountered the evil force from the dawn of time known as Fenric.

The Doctor confronts his old enemy the Master on the planet of the Cheetah People for what may be their ultimate showdown. Many years later, when the Master is exterminated by the Daleks, the arch rival requests that the Doctor take his remains back to Gallifrey. But this is a trap ...

Try these on DVD!

Paradise Towers sees the Doctor and his companion Melanie Bush arrive at a high-rise apartment block sometime in the future. The corridors are covered in graffiti and inhabited by gangs of girls called Kangs and elderly residents called Rezzies. The Chief Caretaker and his men try to keep order. But where is the rest of their society? The Doctor and Mel try to avoid homicidal cleaning robots as they uncover the truth and face the Towers' Great Architect. While not being a big fan favourite, this story marks the start of the series' new production team attempting to freshen up the format.

In *Delta and the Bannermen*, the Doctor and Mel win a holiday to Disneyland in the 1950s but instead end up in a run-down holiday camp in Wales. The Doctor and the humans who run the camp team up with shape-changing aliens called Navarinos to try and save Delta, an alien queen who is on the run from mercenaries, the evil Bannermen. Meanwhile, two bemused American agents are looking for a lost satellite. Very light in tone, this story shows the Doctor's tender side.

Remembrance of the Daleks revisits Coal Hill School, the school attended by the Doctor's granddaughter Susan in the very first *Doctor Who* story in 1963. We discover that the Doctor may be older and more powerful than we had previously suspected, and the story builds on the programme's mythology, introducing a powerful weapon called the Hand of Omega, a new Emperor Dalek and a Special Weapons Dalek. Two Dalek factions battle it out for dominance on the streets of

London and Ace befriends a soldier called Mike, who is not what he seems.

In *The Greatest Show in the Galaxy*, the Doctor wants to visit the infamous Psychic Circus on Segonax, but Ace isn't keen because she is scared of clowns. As various circus acts are ruthlessly obliterated, the Doctor discovers that the show is in fact a front for the ancient Gods of Ragnarok, and he must entertain them if he is to survive. As if that isn't enough, he has the pompous explorer Captain Cook and his assistant Mags to deal with, who has a secret of her own. Due to an asbestos scare at the BBC, many of this story's scenes were shot in a real tent in the car park at the BBC Elstree studios!

Battlefield sees the return of UNIT, the Doctor's old friend Brigadier Alistair Gordon Lethbridge-Stewart and the Third Doctor's beloved car, Bessie. The main villain is Morgaine, who tries to hold up a nuclear missile convoy for her own evil ends. She comes from an alternate dimension where the Doctor is known as Merlin. There's also a stunning new monster called the Destroyer, a demonic figure and arguably one of the best creatures the series ever produced.

In *The Curse of Fenric*, the Doctor and Ace land on the Northumberland coast during the Second World War. Dr Judson is employed by the military to perfect his cipher decoding machine, but an ancient evil is also at work. Individuals and events are manoeuvred so that the device decodes a Viking encryption, releasing Fenric from his bonds. The Time Lord must finish what he started aeons ago.

Survival - The Doctor and Ace arrive in his companion's home suburb of Perivale, London. Residents are disappearing and one of the neighbourhood cats is developing some sinister characteristics. The Doctor finds that the residents are being transported to the planet of the Cheetah People, where he once again encounters the Master, who seems to be developing some feline qualities himself. How will any of them escape the planet's influence and return home?

(This was the very last *Doctor Who* story to be shown by the BBC until the programme returned with the Paul McGann TV movie in 1996. The *Survival* DVD includes a documentary detailing the reasons why the show was taken off air.)

Miscellany

- When BBC Controller Michael Grade decided to axe Colin Baker as the star of *Doctor Who*, the actor was nonetheless asked to return to do the first four-part story of Season 24 and then regenerate. *Time and the Rani* (originally titled *Strange Matter*) was written with Colin Baker in mind and then had to be rejigged when the actor declined to appear. Sylvester McCoy briefly donned a curly wig and Baker's costume to play the injured Sixth Doctor before regenerating into the Seventh.

- As the scripts for his debut season were written before McCoy was cast, the actor was advised to rely on his instincts. He looked to real-life eccentric scientist doctors like David Bellamy and Magnus

Pike for inspiration, as well as his childhood heroes Buster Keaton and the Keystone Cops, resulting in an often zany portrayal. As his first season progressed, the actor found the characterisation that worked best.

- The new Doctor had his work cut out from the start, with his episodes scheduled against the popular soap opera *Coronation Street*. When quizzed about this Jonathan Powell said *Doctor Who* would provide complementary entertainment for younger viewers who tended not to watch the soap. Despite BBC audience figures not including those who recorded the programme on home video, the show still averaged around five million viewers, and gained a million more in the twenty-fifth anniversary year.

- Incoming script editor Andrew Cartmel was brought onto the *Doctor Who* team following the departure of his predecessor Eric Saward, who had had disagreements with producer John Nathan-Turner. Cartmel felt that the series had built up too much mythology and continuity about the Time Lords, and from *Paradise Towers* onwards he sought to refresh the series and return to the idea of the Doctor as a mysterious explorer travelling through time.

- During McCoy's second season, the twenty-fifth anniversary year, Andrew Cartmel sowed the seeds of what some have termed 'the Cartmel Masterplan' – that Omega's experiments gave Gallifrey the power of time travel, that Rassilon established Time Lord society, that a third unnamed figure was their contemporary, and that all three were involved in the Dark Time or Time of Chaos. History came to remember Omega as lost to the world of antimatter, Rassilon became legend, and the Other disappeared. Was 'the Other' the Doctor?

- McCoy's first season of *Doctor Who* saw the debut of a brand new title sequence, the series' first to utilise CGI, designed by Oliver Elmes, who had also created the titles of the popular situation comedy *The Good Life*. Keff McCulloch was asked to provide a new version of the theme music. This was such a radical reinterpretation of the tune that the original theme arranger, Delia Derbyshire, is said to have written to John Nathan-Turner, stating that composer Ron Grainer would be turning in his grave. Nathan-Turner defended McCulloch's version, feeling that it evoked the series' new 'funky' style.

- The Kandy Man, from *The Happiness Patrol*, was to be one of *Doctor Who*'s most controversial monsters. He was originally intended to be a more humanoid figure wearing a white laboratory coat with a confectionary-like complexion, but the special effects team ultimately realised him as a man made out of liquorice allsorts. The similarity to Bertie Bassett, the character used to advertise Bassett's sweets, did not go unnoticed and the company's CEO wrote to the BBC to complain. The BBC insisted there had been no copyright infringement, but pledged that the Kandy Man would never return.

- Season 26, McCoy's third series of *Doctor Who*, opened to the programme's lowest ever ratings, with *Battlefield* part one achieving only 3.1 million viewers. The new season had been barely trailed by BBC One, while ITV were heavily promoting their new third weekly episode of *Coronation Street*. The walls of the TARDIS interior set had been junked and no new set had been commissioned. This resulted in *Battlefield* depicting the control room cloaked in darkness to hide the fact that the makeshift walls were made from cardboard. John Nathan-Turner was told he would be free to work on another project after leaving *Doctor Who*. He sensed the end for the series was nigh.

- In an attempt to make the Doctor's travelling companion more central to the overall narrative, John Nathan-Turner, Andrew Cartmel and scriptwriter Ian Briggs created the character of Ace. Real name Dorothy, a streetwise delinquent from 1980s Perivale, she is whisked away from her humdrum life (although this is not shown on screen) and works as a waitress on Iceworld. Taking her under his wing, the Doctor endeavours to educate her and make her face her fears. By the time we reach the Seventh Doctor's penultimate adventure, *The Curse of Fenric*, it seems she has been a pawn in a much broader game played by the Doctor and an ancient evil force.

- In the final season, the Doctor appears to use 'super' powers, on a couple of occasions disarming villains by placing his finger on their foreheads.

- *Battlefield* would mark Nicholas Courtney's final appearance in the series as Brigadier Lethbridge-Stewart. It was also intended by John Nathan-Turner that the character would die in this story. Later, the producer felt that the story wasn't strong enough for him to go out in a blaze of glory, and the Brigadier lived on. He was told by the Doctor that he would one day die in bed.

- The original script for *Survival* suggested that the Doctor might be more than just a Time Lord, a theme begun in an un-broadcast scene from *Remembrance of the Daleks*, with even the Master seemingly unsure about the Doctor's origins. With the programme's future uncertain, Andrew Cartmel chose to give the story a more upbeat ending instead.

- Sylvester McCoy and Sophie Aldred were to make two further television appearances together following transmission of *Survival*. In 1990 they played their respective characters in a schools programme called *Search Out Science*, and in 1993 they joined other former Doctors and companions in *Dimensions in Time*, a special 3D Adventure for the Children in Need charity. They were also planned to appear in *The Dark Dimension*, a proposed *Doctor Who* thirtieth anniversary special for BBC One with Tom Baker in the main role, but this failed to go ahead, and McCoy alone would return to bow out in the *Doctor Who* TV Movie in 1996.

- When, in 1991, it became obvious *Doctor Who* would not be returning to television any time soon, Virgin Publishing acquired a BBC licence to release full length original novels. The paperback series, *Doctor Who–The New Adventures,* published one book a month and carried on where the TV show left off, with the Seventh Doctor becoming ever more darker and Ace being joined by a specially created-for-the-range companion in the form of thirty-something Professor Bernice Summerfield. By the time the book series reached the events of the 1996 TV movie, the Doctor was travelling alone.

CHAPTER 8

THE WILDERNESS YEARS
Phase 1

1990-1995

In the series of original novels following the cancellation of *Doctor Who* on television, the Doctor continues to be one step ahead of his adversaries, playing them like pawns in a game of chess. A more mature Ace takes his manipulative nature in her stride, while new companion, a thirty-something archaeologist, Professor Bernice 'Benny' Summerfield, plays the traditional companion role. Later, Ace will leave and the Doctor and Benny will be joined by adjudicator Roz Forrester and her partner Chris Cwej. The Time Lord will eventually return to his home on Gallifrey.

Who is the Doctor?

The Doctor's true origins are a mystery. Even the Time Lords might not know who he really is. At the dawn of the universe, sometime between the Big Bang and the establishing of intelligent life on Gallifrey, there were three demigods–Omega, a Gallifreyan who created the means for time travel technology; Rassilon, who organised Time Lord society and became their president; and 'the Other'. Omega and Rassilon went down in history as great legends, while the Other disappeared. Is the Doctor really the Other? He knows a lot more than he lets on. We see him reach one thousand years of age. But maybe even that isn't true ...

Track Down These Novels!

Timewyrm: Exodus. From the pen of original series script editor and writer Terrance Dicks, the Doctor and Ace land in an alternate London in the year 1951, where Adolf Hitler has invaded Britain and seized control. Now the

Union Jack flag has gone and the Nazi swastika is ever present. The change in Earth's history is connected to the War Lord from the Second Doctor's final TV story *The War Games*. This book is the second of the Timewyrm quadrilogy.

Nightshade is the debut novel of Mark Gatiss, and sees the Doctor uncharacteristically pensive and melancholic. Becoming distant, he avoids contact with Ace and wanders the labyrinthine corridors of the TARDIS before taking solace in the isolated village of Crook Marsham in 1968. However, the village is not as idyllic as legend has it, and its populace are being picked off. The novel features the Doctor's granddaughter Susan, and alludes to the First Doctor's departure from Gallifrey.

Love and War is Paul Cornell's second novel in the series and introduces Professor Bernice Summerfield to the range. The Doctor and Ace find themselves on the planet Heaven. It is a world made to suit those who seek a final resting place. Bernice is studying the ancient civilisation which once lived there. The war between Earth, the Draconians and the Daleks mentioned in the Jon Pertwee TV story *Frontier in Space* rages on.

Human Nature by Paul Cornell. The Doctor is being hounded by the Aubertide, a family of alien shape-shifters, and so uses a device to hide his true identity. With his Gallifreyan origins genetically disguised and his real memories suppressed, the Doctor becomes John Smith and teaches at a boys' school in 1913. When the Aubertide track him down, Benny needs to get the Doctor's true self back. But John Smith won't cooperate–

he has fallen in love with the school nurse Joan Redfern ... This is the novel that Cornell would be asked to adapt into the two-part *Human Nature/The Family of Blood* for the revived TV series in 2007.

Blood Heat by Jim Mortimore. The Doctor, Ace and Bernice land on an alternate Earth, where the Silurians defeated the human attempts to suppress them in the 1970 TV story *Doctor Who and the Silurians*, killed the Third Doctor and took over the world. The Brigadier is embittered and hopes to annihilate the Silurians with nuclear bombs. But what happened to the Third Doctor's TARDIS?

Lungbarrow by Marc Platt. The story of the ever enigmatic Seventh Doctor comes to an end in the Virgin Publishing range as he returns to his house on Gallifrey. The secrets of the past are catching up with the Doctor. Is he the mysterious historical figure recalled in legend as The Other?

The Missing Adventures

A complementary series of original novels set in the Doctor's past.

The Plotters by Gareth Roberts, featuring the First Doctor, Vicky, Ian and Barbara. The TARDIS lands in the year 1605. Vicky disguises herself as a boy in the court of King James I. But for Barbara, her loyalties and her knowledge of England's history are put to the test when she falls in love with Guy Fawkes.

The Romance of Crime by Gareth Roberts, featuring the Fourth Doctor, the Second Romana and K9. The TARDIS lands on the Rock of Judgement: a court, prison and place of execution. There they become embroiled in an investigation by the system's finest lawman. What connects the macabre gallery of artist Menlove Stokes with the slaughter of a survey team on a distant planet?

Cold Fusion by Lance Parkin, featuring the Fifth Doctor, Adric, Tegan and Nyssa, and the Seventh Doctor, Chris and Roz. The Fifth Doctor and his companions arrive on an ice planet run by the Scientifica. There he finds a terribly emaciated woman close to death. As she gradually recovers, she appears to be of Time Lord origin. Is she the Doctor's wife from the time before he fled Gallifrey? Meanwhile, the Seventh Doctor and his companions arrive. How will he cope when he meets Adric again, knowing the boy's fate?

Miscellany

• When it became patently obvious that *Doctor Who* would not be returning to television any time soon, fan and publisher Peter Darvill-Evans at Virgin Publishing Ltd approached the BBC to acquire a licence to produce full length novels aimed at adults who had grown up watching the programme. The Corporation seemed to care little about the character's future and granted Virgin a licence rather than looking into producing a literary range of their own. Darvill-Evans invited TV scribes like Terrance Dicks and Andrew Cartmel to contribute, as well as debut fan authors like John Peel, Paul Cornell, Gareth

Roberts, Lance Parkin, Jim Mortimore, Marc Platt and Mark Gatiss, to name a few. *Doctor Who–The New Adventures* launched in 1991 with *Timewyrm: Genesys* by John Peel. The range published one book a month and won high acclaim in the sci-fi press.

- After the initial run, Rebecca Levene was appointed range editor and developed the series with the writers. While Sylvester McCoy's performance on television always met with a mixed response, his characterisation of the Seventh Doctor worked very well in print, as the team focused on the darker Doctor that Andrew Cartmel had been pushing for in the final season of the television programme. The concept of the Doctor being part of an ancient mysterious Time Lord triumvirate was continued and Paul Cornell labelled him 'Time's Champion'.

- Mark Gatiss, whose debut novel was *Nightshade*, would go on to enjoy great acclaim as a star and co-creator of the macabre BBC Two comedy *The League of Gentlemen*, pen further adventures in original *Doctor Who* novels and on audio, before writing and appearing in a number of *Doctor Who* television episodes from 2005 onwards.

- As the character Ace was being phased out, Paul Cornell was invited to create a new companion for the range. Professor Bernice Summerfield was a thirty-something beer-swilling archaeologist and was unlike the stereotypical companions of the television series.

- The Doctor reaches one thousand years of age in Kate Orman's *Set Piece*.

- By the show's thirty-first year, 1994, the Virgin series was so popular that a secondary range was launched. Entitled *The Missing Adventures*, each of its novels existed in the TV series' past, slotting stories into the existing canon of adventures and featuring one of the first six Doctors and their companions. This range became popular quickly, upping its output to one book a month.

- When BBC Worldwide struck a deal with Universal Television to produce a TV movie starring Paul McGann as the Eighth Doctor, Virgin's licence was unceremoniously revoked. Having left Virgin Publishing to it for a good six years to develop and nurture a loyal fan following, the Corporation determined to inherit the readership by launching their own ranges–the Eighth Doctor Adventures and the Past Doctor Adventures–to be published by BBC Books, one of each a month.

- Virgin's final book in *The New Adventures* range was *The Dying Days* by Lance Parkin, featuring the Eighth Doctor from the TV Movie.

- Determined to continue, Rebecca Levene and her team of writers dropped the *Doctor Who* logo and the character of the Doctor and continued *The New Adventures* range with Professor Bernice Summerfield and characters specifically created for the novel series. The Benny books lasted until 1999.

Thirty Years in the TARDIS

To celebrate the thirtieth anniversary of *Doctor Who* in 1993, BBC One controller Alan Yentob commissioned an hour-long documentary entitled *Thirty Years in the TARDIS*. For many fans, this was the first time many had seen the likes of Verity Lambert, Barry Letts, Terrance Dicks and Eric Saward interviewed on camera. Directed by lifelong fan and BBC employee Kevin Davies, the documentary featured all the surviving actors to have played the Doctor, a plethora of companions and a great many clips. Celebrity fans were also interviewed and specially shot re-enactments illustrated the appeal of the series. The programme climaxed with a tongue-in-cheek scene where Alan Yentob is pressured to confirm rumours that the BBC is in talks with Steven Spielberg's company Amblin about the future of the series.

Miscellany

- BBC Video released an extended version as *More Than Thirty Years in the TARDIS* in 1994. It is now available on DVD in the box set *The Legacy Collection*.

CHAPTER 9

THE DOCTOR
As played by
Paul McGann

1996 and 2013

The Eighth Doctor is the most romantic incarnation of the Time Lord so far, and is the first to engage in a romantic relationship (although previous Doctors had not been above the occasional flirt!). He clearly has feelings for the beautiful Doctor Grace Holloway, who attempts to save his life, and he is keen for her to join him on his travels, although she ultimately decides not to. Handsome and dashing with a shock of dark hair, the new Doctor adapts a Wild Bill Hickok fancy dress costume (minus the hat and holster) to create a Byronesque image.

Proving he can handle a motorbike, this Doctor appears to have some of the Third Doctor's love of action whilst also displaying the youthful sensitivity and dry wit of the Fifth incarnation. He has a tendency to drop hints to people about things that might happen in their future, something that previous Doctors had refrained from doing, and takes pleasure from the small things in life, such as a pair of shoes that fit his feet perfectly.

Whereas the Fifth Doctor had given his life to save a friend, the Eighth Doctor is perhaps even more brave and noble and ultimately gave his to save a total stranger.

Who is the Doctor?

The regeneration of the Seventh Doctor into the Eighth was unusual in that the Doctor actually appeared to die prior to transforming, whereas previously he had only been injured, albeit severely. We discover that the Master has survived the passing of his stolen body by occupying that of a shape-shifting serpentine alien. The Doctor appears to be half-human (possibly on his mother's side, although he may claim this in jest) and recalls spending time on Gallifrey with his father.

Unlike previous Doctors, this incarnation seems willing to change time and does so to save the lives of Grace Holloway and Change Lee, something the Fifth Doctor had been unprepared to do for Adric.

Later, the Time War breaks out between the Daleks and the Time Lords. The Doctor ultimately crash-lands on Karn and perishes, but is revived by the Sisterhood of Karn, who provide an elixir to trigger his regeneration, giving him a degree of choice in the new body he will take. In order to participate in the Time War, which threatens all reality, the Doctor chooses to take the form of a warrior...

Try these on DVD!

Doctor Who the TV Movie–San Francisco 1999. The Seventh Doctor arrives in the TARDIS and is gunned down by a gang of youths in a hail of bullets. He is rushed to hospital, where Doctor Grace Holloway tries in vain to save him, confused by his unique anatomy. The hospital staff are stunned when the Doctor appears to be resurrected and Grace finds that the intriguing stranger is not the man he once was. Meanwhile, having shed his shape-shifting body in favour of seizing that of paramedic Bruce, the Master befriends the young Chang Lee and captures the Doctor's TARDIS, which he claims actually belongs to him. But he wants something more-the Doctor's remaining lives. With the fate of the Earth at stake on New Year's Eve, the Doctor needs a beryllium atomic clock to put things right or the entire planet may be sucked into the Eye of Harmony ...

The Day of the Doctor - This DVD contains the mini-adventure *The Night of the Doctor*, in which the Eighth

Doctor encounters the Sisterhood of Karn and regenerates into the War Doctor, played by John Hurt. Out in space, the Doctor tries to rescue a pilot called Cass, whose spacecraft is about to crash. Realising that he is a Time Lord and therefore may be partly responsible for the Time War, Cass refuses the Doctor's help, but he will not abandon her and the two are killed when the ship crashes on Karn. The Sisterhood of Karn resurrect the Doctor and tell him the Time War threatens all reality. They ask him not to allow the universe to fall, as it stands 'on the brink'. The Doctor agrees to drink a potion provided by the Sisterhood and regenerates into a new body, who declares himself 'Doctor no more.'

Despite his short tenure on television, the Eighth Doctor has enjoyed a new lease of life on audio. The company Big Finish Productions began producing full cast *Doctor Who* stories on CD in 1999. Paul McGann reprised the role of the Doctor in 2001. Some of his audio adventures have been transmitted on BBC Radio.

Miscellany

- Executive Producer Philip Segal had originally hoped to produce a full series of Eighth Doctor episodes, but failed to get the support of the American networks and chose to make a TV Movie instead. He hoped the movie would act as a 'backdoor pilot', but although the film did well in Britain, getting over nine million viewers, it was not sufficiently popular in the US to result in a series. Segal had originally intended to produce *Doctor Who* for Steven Spielberg's production company Amblin, but by the time the movie was made, Amblin were no longer involved in the deal, and the film was ultimately a co-production between BBC Worldwide and Universal Studios for the Fox Network. The movie had a budget of $5 million.

- The script for the movie was written by British writer Matthew Jacobs, a man with a unique link to *Doctor Who*–his father Anthony Jacobs had played the role of Doc Holliday in the William Hartnell story *The Gunfighters*, and the young Matthew had visited the studio during production. The man chosen to direct the story was yet another Brit, in the form of Geoffrey Sax, who had worked on popular UK series *The New Statesman*, *Spitting Image* and *Bergerac*.

- The story ultimately used for the TV Movie was a continuation of the original BBC series, with the Seventh Doctor played by Sylvester McCoy regenerating into the Eighth Doctor on screen. This was not always the intention, and earlier proposed storylines by John Leekley and Robert DeLaurentis had very much been 'reboots' featuring a young version of the Doctor before he had left Gallifrey. Had the proposed series gone down the reboot route, it would appear that classic *Doctor Who* stories such as *Tomb of the Cybermen* and *Earthshock* might have been remade–certainly this was the impression given in the series 'bible' prepared for prospective writers, although the older stories were arguably outlined in the bible to illustrate the massive storytelling potential of the *Doctor Who* format.

- Numerous actors were considered to play the role of the Eighth Doctor. Philip Segal was keen on former Monty Python star Michael Palin and also discussed the role with actor Michael Crawford, who had found fame in the popular British sitcom *Some Mothers Do 'Ave 'Em* . Another Python, Eric Idle, was also rumoured. Perhaps the most bizarre name to be linked with the role was *Baywatch* star David Hasselhoff! Numerous actors screen-tested for the part, including John Sessions, Tony Slattery, Liam Cunningham and Paul McGann's brother, Mark.

• The man ultimately chosen to play the new Doctor, thirty-six-year-old actor Paul McGann, was part of a family of acting brothers, and had made his name in quality BBC dramas such as *The Monocled Mutineer* and cult films like *Withnail and I*. It would seem that McGann was less sure of himself than the producers. In an interview published in *TV Times*, issue dated 25-31 May 1996, he would say, 'When I saw the casting agent in Los Angeles, I kept saying "You've got the wrong fella." Other actors seemed to fit the image better, so I turned it down'.

• The actor Gordon Tipple is credited as playing the 'Old Master' in the movie. In fact, he appears only very briefly in the opening credits. He was originally to have provided the movie's opening monologue, but it was ultimately decided that this would be narrated by Paul McGann as the Doctor instead.

• The main role of the Master was played by Eric Roberts, brother of famous film actress Julia Roberts.

• The movie contained many elements familiar to *Doctor Who* fans. The original theme music was retained (albeit as a new orchestral arrangement from composer John Debney) and the opening titles were similar to those seen during Tom Baker's time on the programme. Although the title sequence continued the theme of a time tunnel, the titles broke tradition by not including the Doctor's face (the first time this had happened since the Hartnell era). Instead, the sequence featured the names of the main cast, setting a precedent for the 2005 relaunch. The TARDIS remained a police box (actually one of the most faithful reproductions of a police box ever seen in *Doctor Who*) and the interior was a stunning piece of set design–far bigger than the console room seen in the original series and very much in the 'retro' style of a spaceship from a Jules Verne novel. The *Doctor Who* logo was a modified version of that used for the bulk of the Pertwee era and has since been used on the majority of *Doctor Who* merchandise based on the classic series. There were some things that did not please fans, such as the TARDIS chameleon circuit being referred to as a 'cloaking device,' the Doctor apparently being half-human and the Eye of Harmony being in the TARDIS rather than on Gallifrey as we had previously seen in the Fourth Doctor story *The Deadly Assassin*.

- For the first time since the Peter Davison story *The Visitation* in 1982, the Doctor is once again seen using his sonic screwdriver.

- Paul McGann was concerned about being the first Doctor to share an on-screen kiss, telling *The Sun* newspaper: 'I kept my lips together when I kissed Daphne (Ashbrook) because I didn't want the love scenes to be too sexy … I didn't want to do anything that might upset a family audience.'

• The movie was the first *Doctor Who* story to be filmed in North America and remains the only one to be mounted entirely outside of the UK.

• Paul McGann humorously boasts that he is both the longest and shortest-serving actor in the role of the Doctor. He has the least amount of screen time, but the most time elapsed between him taking the role and his successor, Christopher Eccleston, beginning his tenure.

• The British transmission of the story was dedicated to Third Doctor Jon Pertwee, who had died shortly before the move was shown.

• The movie was broadcast on 12 May 1996 in the USA and 27 May in the UK. It was promoted under the tag line 'He's back and it's about time'. The video was supposed to be released in the UK well in advance of the TV screening, but the tragic shootings in Dunblane meant that gun-related scenes in the film had to be cut, and it was finally released on 22 May. The movie was not a huge success in the United States (being broadcast opposite the last ever episode of popular comedy series *Roseanne*) and did not gain high enough ratings to justify the commissioning of a series. Ironically, it did very well in the UK, gaining over 9 million viewers but, as it was a co-production, all parties concerned would have had to be in agreement for the series to continue.

• BBC Books published a novelisation of the story by Gary Russell.

- There was another lease of life for McGann's Doctor from the BBC–a *Radio Times* comic strip based on the movie ran for forty-two issues of the magazine from June 1996 to March 1997.

- In *The Night of the Doctor*, the Doctor mentions his companions from the Big Finish audio stories, the first time that the audios had been recognised as part of the official *Doctor Who* 'canon'. The story was an Internet sensation, with 2.5 million views in the week of its release.

CHAPTER 10

THE WILDERNESS YEARS
Phase 2

1996-2005

The Eighth Doctor travels alone until the TARDIS returns to the junkyard on Totter's Lane, as seen in *An Unearthly Child*. In 1997, the young Samantha 'Sam' Jones joins him. Later, his companions are Fitz, Compassion (a human TARDIS), a third regeneration of Romana, Anji Kapoor and Trix.

Who is the Doctor?

Still the dashing adventurer of the 1996 TV Movie, the Doctor has second sight when it comes to obscure future details in the lives of those with whom he comes into contact. The notion that the Doctor is half-human (introduced in the movie) is politely ignored.

Track down these novels!

The Eight Doctors by Terrance Dicks. The Master has left one final booby trap in the TARDIS, which takes away the Doctor's memories. He must visit key moments in his own past and confront his former incarnations to find himself again.

Alien Bodies by Lawrence Miles. Set on an island in the East Indies, this story features old enemies and fresh concepts that take the series forward. The novel has been highly praised for its inventiveness.

Interference - books one and two by Lawrence Miles. A continuity-laden story in which the Doctor's personal history is rewritten by a Time Lord cult called Faction Paradox, resulting in an alternate regeneration for the Third Doctor.

In addition to BBC Books' Eighth Doctor Adventures, there were the Past Doctor Adventures.

Players by Terrance Dicks, featuring the Sixth Doctor and Peri. A group of shadowy players delight in altering the personal history of one Winston Churchill. The Doctor encounters him in the Boer War before his political career is established and determines to put his role in the world's affairs back on track. Very well-written, the Sixth Doctor comes across vividly. The book was republished in 2013 as part of the series' fiftieth anniversary celebrations.

Illegal Alien by Mike Tucker and Robert Perry, featuring the Seventh Doctor and Ace. Told through the eyes of American private eye Cody McBride and set in Second World War London. The Cybermen are taking advantage of death being on streets and building their army. The Nazis, meanwhile, are set on acquiring their technology to give them the upper hand in the war. This book was republished in 2014.

The Infinity Doctors by Lance Parkin, featuring an undefined Doctor on Gallifrey. Big ideas and well-written prose hint at where our hero might have come from and where he might end up. The author doesn't reveal which incarnation it is, whether the events are in the Doctor's past or future–it's a great treat for fans and was published to mark *Doctor Who*'s thirty-fifth anniversary in 1998.

Miscellany

- Duplicating the format created and developed by Virgin Publishing, BBC Books launched the dual range of novels–the Eighth Doctor Adventures and the Past Doctor Adventures.

- Initially the ranges were overseen by Nuala Buffini before *Doctor Who* fan and popular children's author Stephen Cole took the reins.

- The 2011 television story *The Doctor's Wife* by Neil Gaiman, in which the TARDIS takes on human form and occupies the body of a woman named Idris, while being highly praised by fans and critics alike, was not a completely original concept. A human-like female becoming a TARDIS had been a running storyline in the EDAs. In those, she was called Compassion.

- In the EDAs, the Doctor sets off a sequence of events that result in Gallifrey and the Time Lords being erased from history. This idea would be picked up by Russell T Davies in 2005 and form a major plotline in his new television series of *Doctor Who*.

- The Eighth Doctor continued his adventures in book form between 1996 and 2005. When the television series returned in 2005, the Eighth Doctor was redefined as part of the 'classic series' canon.

Doctor Who – the Full Cast Audio Adventures released on CD and for download by Big Finish Productions.

The Sirens of Time by Nicholas Briggs, starring Peter Davison, Colin Baker and Sylvester McCoy as the Doctor. Gallifrey is threatened by a fleet of warships, and someone is trying to erase the Doctor. His fifth, sixth and seventh incarnations are confronted individually and then the Doctors join forces to thwart the enemy.

Phantasmagoria by Mark Gatiss, starring Peter Davison as the Doctor with Mark Strickson as Turlough. In London 1702 Sir Nikolas Valentine runs the Diabola Club, where individuals mysteriously disappear after losing a game of cards.

The Genocide Machine by Mike Tucker, starring Sylvester McCoy as the Doctor with Sophie Aldred as Ace. Set on the tropical world of Kar-Charrat, where the Daleks are intent on acquiring the properties of a technological feat called the Wetworks Facility.

The Marian Conspiracy by Jacqueline Raynor, starring Colin Baker as the Doctor and introducing Maggie Stables as Dr Evelyn Smythe. Investigating why his new friend Evelyn is fading from time, the Doctor traces the cause back to the era of Queen Mary.

The Shadow of the Scourge by Paul Cornell, starring Sylvester McCoy as the Doctor, Sophie Aldred as Ace with Lisa Bowerman as Professor Bernice Summerfield. The first Big Finish play to be set in the universe of the Virgin *New Adventures*. Author Paul Cornell has said that the Scourge are representative of his own battle with depression.

The Holy Terror by Robert Shearman, starring Colin Baker as the Doctor and Robert Jezek as Frobisher. Set in a castle where a bizarre power struggle is under way, the story looks at strict adherence to traditions and customs, and a very dark father/son relationship. Frobisher was a popular companion to the Sixth Doctor in the *Doctor Who Magazine* comic strips. He was a shape-shifting alien who settled on the form of a penguin. This was the first time the character was brought to life by an actor.

Jubilee by Robert Shearman, starring Colin Baker as the Doctor with Maggie Stables as Evelyn. Separated from the TARDIS and stranded in an alternate timeline where England is the English Empire and rules the world after the Dalek war of 1903, the Doctor finds that the last surviving Dalek is being tortured by President Rochester for propaganda purposes. This story was heavily reworked and screened in the revived 2005 television series as *Dalek*.

The Spectre of Lanyon Moor by Nicholas Pegg, starring Colin Baker as the Doctor with Maggie Stables as Evelyn and Nicholas Courtney as Brigadier Lethbridge-Stewart. An ancient evil plagues the moors of Cornwall. The Doctor and Evelyn join forces with the Brigadier to defeat it.

Davros by Lance Parkin, starring Colin Baker as the Doctor and Terry Molloy as Davros. Separated from the Daleks and vulnerable, the evil genius agrees to work for an Earth corporation on famine relief. The Doctor doesn't trust him at all, and is more than a little appalled when he is forced to work alongside him. What is Davros really up to?

Dust Breeding by Mike Tucker, starring Sylvester McCoy as the Doctor, Sophie Aldred as Ace and Geoffrey Beevers as The Master. In a base on the distant barren world Duchamp 331, an evil force appears to be connected to the famous painting The Scream, by Edvard Munch. Since actor Anthony Ainley turned down invitations to reprise the role of the Master, Big Finish approached his predecessor Geoffrey Beevers (who only played the character in one TV story, *The Keeper of Traken*). In this adventure, he returns with great relish.

Storm Warning by Alan Barnes, starring Paul McGann as the Doctor and introducing India Fisher as Charlotte 'Charley' Pollard. The story is set on the doomed World War Two airship R101, where the Doctor is joined by a young Edwardian adventuress. But events don't play out the way history says they should. What has Charley's presence there got to do with it?

The Chimes of Midnight by Robert Shearman, starring Paul McGann as the Doctor with India Fisher as Charley Pollard. Our heroes appear to have arrived inside an Edwardian house where, at the stroke of midnight, one of the inhabitants gets murdered. But as several of them are bumped off, the first to die come back. What is going on, and where is the house really?

Zagreus by Alan Barnes, starring Peter Davison, Colin Baker, Sylvester McCoy and Paul McGann as the Doctor. A strange and complex tale, in which the Doctor is taken over by a character from an ancient Gallifreyan nursery rhyme. The setting affords all the Big Finish Doctors to meet one another. Snippets of Jon Pertwee's voice from an unofficial fan-made production are woven in. As was his custom until 2013, Tom Baker declined to appear.

Miscellany

- In 1998, audio producers/writers Gary Russell and Nicholas Briggs joined forces with Jason Haigh-Ellery, who owned the company Big Finish Productions. With John Ainsworth acting as PR, the company approached Rebecca Levene at Virgin Publishing to acquire a licence to make full cast audio plays of the Bernice Summerfield *New Adventures* novels. The audios, released straight to CD, were high-quality radio plays with sound effects and music, and guest starred actors from the *Doctor Who* TV series. Lisa Bowerman, who starred as Kara the Cheetah Person in the final televised adventure, was cast as Benny.

- With a number of Benny plays under their belt and high acclaim in the sci-fi journals, Big Finish approached Steve Cole at BBC Worldwide to see if the Corporation would licence their company to produce *Doctor Who* on audio. With no sign of a new television series on the horizon and no interest in the franchise at BBC Radio, a licence was granted. Nicholas Briggs wrote and directed *The Sirens of Time*. It was produced as a four-part serial in the style of the original show. Sylvester McCoy was the Doctor in the first episode, followed by Peter Davison in the second and Colin Baker in the third. The concluding episode saw the three Doctors joining forces to defeat their common enemy.

- The Terry Nation Estate granted the company the rights to use the Daleks in their series. Nicholas

Briggs voiced the creatures in the style of the 1960s Dalek movies starring Peter Cushing as Dr. Who. Sound effects included key sounds from the television series and the movies.

- Davison, Baker and McCoy signed up to reprise their respective roles immediately in 1999. Tom Baker declined the offer to bring back the Fourth Doctor (until he was eventually persuaded in 2012 by Leela actress Louise Jameson) and Paul McGann did not participate until 2001. Since Universal Television owned the rights to TV Movie companions Grace Holloway and Chang Lee, Big Finish created the character of Charley Pollard and cast India Fisher to star opposite McGann.

- BBC Radio commissioned Big Finish to make some stories especially for broadcast on BBC Radio 7. In these, Paul McGann was joined by Sheridan Smith as new companion Lucie Miller.

- All of the living actors to have played the Doctor in the classic series appeared in the fiftieth anniversary special *The Light at the End* by Nicholas Briggs. The first three Doctors were represented in cameo scenes by soundalike actors.

- When Russell T Davies headed up the new television series of *Doctor Who* in 2003, the BBC revoked all the licences so that merchandise could be exclusively controlled by the Corporation. Knowing the role Big Finish had played in keeping *Doctor Who* alive, Davies told fellow executive producer Mal Young that he would deal with the company. Young had no knowledge of Big Finish, so Davies discreetly told them not to worry–their licence would be renewed and they would represent the classic series Doctors on audio, while the revived TV series and BBC Books focused exclusively on the Ninth Doctor as played by Christopher Eccleston.

CHAPTER 11

THE DOCTOR
As played by
Christopher Eccleston

2005

When he first appears, the Ninth Doctor is more distant, reticent and harder–a real mystery. All of the flamboyance and eccentric whims of his previous selves seem absent. He has short cropped hair, black trousers, a thin dark jumper and a weathered black leather jacket. He may have only recently regenerated or he might have been travelling for some time. One thing is certain, though–he has been travelling alone.

In addition to his sonic screwdriver (which appears to have greater powers than before), the Doctor now makes use of psychic paper in the form of a pass that causes authority figures to think whatever the Doctor wants them to, thus enabling him to go anywhere he likes unchallenged.

His arrival on contemporary Earth is connected with another attempt by the Nestene Consciousness to take over the world using living plastic. He has no intentions of befriending the young Rose Tyler after rescuing her from Autons masquerading as shop mannequins in the basement of the department store where she works. But from then on, their lives are intertwined. He wants to show her all of time and space. By their third adventure, there appears to be a bigger picture unfolding, something that involves them both, and the phrase 'Bad Wolf' is uttered for the first time.

As their friendship blossoms, the Doctor's character loses its edge; he shows signs of becoming more like his old selves. But when the Bad Wolf prophecy reaches fulfilment, the Doctor must be willing sacrifice everything to save his dear friend.

Who is the Doctor?

In his first episode, the Doctor catches sight of himself in a mirror. He thinks his appearance isn't bad–shame about the ears–but it could be worse. Is he talking about a recent haircut or his regeneration?

He is at first reluctant to accept Rose as his travelling companion, telling her to go home. When he gives in to his loneliness and takes her five million years into the future to witness the destruction of Earth, he confesses that his own planet burned in a Time War between the Time Lords and the Daleks. They virtually wiped one another out. He is the sole survivor of his race–the last of the Time Lords. Did he do something drastic to bring an end to the conflict, something terrible?

When encountering the last surviving Dalek, he seems ready to kill it so as to prevent the creatures ever returning. And his motives in dispensing with villains are called into question when he holds Margaret Blaine (a Slitheen) prisoner in the TARDIS.

The Doctor's joy is reignited when he manages to use an alien 'hospital' ship to heal zombie-like residents of London's Second World War Blitz, and for once *everybody* lives.

Then the unthinkable happens–the resurgence of his deadliest enemies, the Daleks. Far off in Earth's future they are set to 'harvest' humankind. His plan to defeat them will result in his own certain death. Maybe it's time, he wonders.

When Rose taps into the time vortex and is turned into a powerful goddess, there is only one way the Doctor can save her from being consumed by it ...

Try These On DVD!

These stories are available as 'vanilla' releases (three episodes per disc with no extra features) or in the Ninth Doctor box set (released as Series One in the UK and Europe and Season One in the United States).

Rose - A young woman is startled when shop window mannequins come alive. She is rescued by a man calling himself the Doctor. Investigating her saviour, she finds that he's a time traveller from another world. Together they confront the Nestene Consciousness and its Autons. Rose abandons her boyfriend Mickey and her mother Jackie to take up the invitation of travelling with the Doctor. Devised and written by the award-winning Russell T Davies, *Doctor Who* was well and truly back!

The End of the World - Five million years in the future, space station Platform One plays host to the destruction of planet Earth, as the sun expands and engulfs the now empty world. A number of aliens have been invited to attend and witness the death. These include Jabe from the Forest of Cheem, the Moxx of Balhoon, the Face of Boe, and the last ever human to be born on Earth, Cassandra–a talking piece of skin stretched across a trampoline-like frame (due to expensive plastic surgery!). One of the delegates is a murderer.

In *The Unquiet Dead*, the Doctor takes Rose to Victorian Cardiff, where Charles Dickens is giving one of his famous readings. Meanwhile, at a funeral parlour, cadavers are coming to life and roaming the streets. How are they connected to the Gelth, and how is young

Gwyneth implicated? With the help of Dickens, the time travellers find out.

Returning Rose to her housing estate in the two-part *Aliens of London/World War Three*, the Doctor finds that they have been gone from the lives of Mickey and Jackie for a whole year (and not twelve days as he'd promised!). London is in crisis when an alien spacecraft plummets from the sky, out of control, and hits Big Ben before crashing into the River Thames. The occupant is a small porcine creature. But it's a genetically engineered decoy. The real enemy are the Slitheen, who have hollowed out the bodies of key government officials so they can assume their identities ...

Dalek - The TARDIS lands in an underground museum in Utah. Its proprietor, Henry van Statten, can't get one of his alien exhibits to talk. He's tried everything from polite conversation to torture. The Doctor thinks he can help, until he finds out what the alien is–the last remaining Dalek. Using cells from Rose's hand, the creature is able to restore itself. But as it endeavours to reach the surface, it finds it has acquired from Rose's DNA graft more than just regenerative properties. It starts to develop human feelings.

In *The Long Game*, the Doctor and Rose land on news station Satellite 5, orbiting Earth at a point in time where homo sapiens are enjoying the Fourth Great and Bountiful Human Empire. Individuals may have information beamed directly into their brains after a special adaptor has been applied to the forehead. This can be opened at the click of their fingers. The very best journalists are invited to join a mysterious elite on Floor 500. But who or what is controlling the station's broadcasts, and to what end?

Knowing the TARDIS can take her to any point in time, Rose is desperate to see her dad in *Father's Day*. He died when she was a child. The Doctor agrees she can see her dad, on the condition that they observe but don't become involved. However, once Rose reaches the point where her father is going to be killed in a road accident, she rushes across the road and drags him to safety. The change in history unleashes dragon creatures called Reapers, which will 'cleanse' the world of humans to sterilise the time paradox. Locked inside a church, Rose realises that her dad Pete Tyler is not the hero she imagined—until it dawns on him that the whole catastrophe has occurred because he didn't die. This is one of the rare truly emotional episodes of *Doctor Who*.

The Empty Child/The Doctor Dances - This two-part adventure starts with the Doctor and Rose pursuing a hospital ship through the time vortex. They arrive in the London Blitz of World War Two. There, the residents of England's capital city are haunted by a gas masked little boy who keeps asking, 'Are you my mummy?' Soon others begin to 'grow' gas masks and behave in the same way. Meanwhile, Rose is saved by a man who appears to be an American captain, Jack Harkness—until she finds herself in his spaceship. Jack is little more than a conman from the fifty-first century. But what has he to do with London's zombies?

In *Boom Town* the Doctor, Rose, Mickey and Captain Jack are resting in Cardiff Bay. There is a huge energy source created by an invisible space-time wormhole, and by parking the TARDIS on top of it, the Doctor's craft can absorb the radiation and use it as fuel. But someone else is also aware of the Bay's unique properties. One Margaret Blaine (the only surviving Slitheen from *World War Three*) has her own ideas on how to exploit it. Capturing her is one thing, but unable to leave immediately, the Doctor will have to deal with the moral dilemma of 'playing god' with the lives of others and witnessing the consequences of his meddling.

The season two-part finale *Bad Wolf/The Parting of the Ways* sees the TARDIS returning to Satellite 5 some one hundred years after the events of *The Long Game*; it is now the control centre for all of Earth's entertainment shows. The Doctor lands in an episode of reality TV show *Big Brother*, while Rose finds herself in a lethal version of *The Weakest Link*. Meanwhile, Jack must deal with killer fashion robots. But the whole broadcasting station is a sham, a diversion cloaking the resurgence of a very real and terrible threat–the Daleks. Harvesting the dregs of humanity, the metal fascists have acquired a religious sensibility. Their emperor is God, and they intend to 'cleanse' Earth and make it their paradise. The situation is beyond even the Doctor's capabilities. He believes he will die in the final showdown.

Miscellany

- Writer Russell T Davies had won multiple awards for his ITV and Channel Four Television series *The Grand*,

Queer as Folk, *Bob and Rose* and *The Second Coming*. The BBC were eager for him to write something for them. Knowing the leverage he now had within the industry, whenever BBC One Controller Lorraine Heggessey suggested he write for the Corporation, Davies said he was only interested in writing *Doctor Who*. In 2003, Heggessey investigated who currently held the rights to the franchise. BBC Films had the rights, but nothing was being developed–apart from a few script treatments, nothing was under way, no actors had been cast. BBC Films released the rights back to BBC Television. Towards the end of the year, the media were informed that Russell T Davies had been commissioned to write and executive produce a new thirteen episode series of *Doctor Who*. The announcement that Christopher Eccleston had been cast as the Doctor was made in March 2004.

• Shortly after the new series was announced, Michael Grade left Channel Four and returned to the BBC. Russell T Davies and BBC Head of Drama, Jane Tranter, are on record as stating that a representative of Grade's arrived at their production office to see how established the production of *Doctor Who* was. It was clear that Grade intended to put a halt to the show's revival. Although nothing had yet been filmed, Tranter says she lied to the rep and said production was well underway and couldn't be stopped. Several weeks into the 2005 broadcast, Michael Grade declared at a press call that he had a confession to make–he and his little boy were watching *Doctor Who* every Saturday.

- Episodes were now forty-five minutes in length. Most stories were self-contained single instalments; a few were two-part adventures.

- In the first episode, Rose comments on the Doctor's apparent north England accent, to which he replies, 'Every planet has a north.'

- No one in the BBC or on the production team knew how the series would be received, and so everyone involved was contracted for just one year. But the first episode was watched by over ten million viewers, with subsequent instalments averaging eight million. Julie Gardner, Head of Drama for BBC Wales (the arm of the Corporation making the show), wasted no time in commissioning a second series.

- Special effects team The Mill created a twisting CGI time vortex for the title sequence. Influenced by the Bernard Lodge sequence from the 1970s, the TARDIS tumbled down it and the new logo flipped into view. The Doctor's face did not feature in it. However, the names of stars Christopher Eccleston and Billie Piper did.

- Russell T Davies initially asked composer Murray Gold to remaster the Delia Derbyshire/BBC Radiophonic Workshop version of Ron Grainer's theme music. But no matter how much he tried, Gold couldn't get it to match the contemporary standard. In the end, he created a new piece of music from scratch. Researching how Delia Derbyshire came up with the original radiophonic sounds, Murray Gold remade them and backed them with an orchestral arrangement. Delia's sounds included the electronic sting or 'scream', the familiar rhythm (which Gold changed to a different sound halfway through), the opening notes of the theme, the organ, and the closing sound. Enhancing these were orchestral strings and brass. Since Russell T Davies was something of a technophobe, Gold had to play the new version to him down the phone. He reported that Russell was so moved he cried.

- The new police box prop was taller and wider than any of the previous versions. A fan animation on YouTube places the different sizes alongside a real police box to demonstrate that none of them have been entirely accurate.

- The new TARDIS interior was designed by Ed Thomas. Russell T Davies and series producer Phil Collinson felt it should be just one room, 'a campervan TARDIS', given that the Doctor had been travelling alone. That said, it was implied in the scripts that there were other rooms. The console was a circular hub rather than six-sided, and the column was connected to the ceiling as in the *TV Movie*. The wall roundels were considerably smaller than on the original series version and the walls had a coral finish, suggesting that the ship had been grown rather than built. In a throwback to the 1960s *Dr. Who* movies starring Peter Cushing, the police box doors were visible from the interior of the ship. It was felt this would complete the illusion that the huge room was inside the telephone box.

- Nicholas Briggs, a lifelong Dalek obsessive, was thrilled to be invited to provide the voices of the Doctor's deadliest enemies. For some years Briggs had been voicing the Daleks on Big Finish audios.

- Despite claiming to be nine hundred and fifty-three in *Time and the Rani* (1987) and possibly ancient in *Remembrance of the Daleks* and *Silver Nemesis* (1988), then claiming to be one thousand in the Virgin novel *Set Piece*, the Doctor in 2005's *Aliens of London* declared himself nine hundred years old.

- The BBC wanted Davies to write all of the thirteen episodes himself so they could pitch the show as his series for them, but in the end they agreed he would plan the series treatment, write the bulk of the episodes (1, 2, 4, 5, 7, 11, 12 and 13) himself, and farm out some of the others to high profile *Doctor Who* fans who were also experienced television scriptwriters. Mark Gatiss wrote *The Unquiet Dead*, Paul Cornell penned *Father's Day*, and Steven Moffat wrote *The Empty Child* and *The Doctor Dances*. Gatiss and Cornell had previously contributed to the Virgin Publishing range and Big Finish Productions when the television series was off the air. *Dalek* by Robert Sherman was adapted from his Big Finish Sixth Doctor audio play *Jubilee*.

- The 'Bad Wolf' thread running through the season was made little of until the final two episodes, as Davies believed that a complex story arc would alienate casual viewers who did not watch every single episode. Similar reasoning led to him vetoing unnecessary references to the classic series.

- To launch the new series, the BBC ran a special trailer in which the Doctor invites the audience, 'Do you wanna come with me?' After showing clips from various episodes, he stands alongside Rose and declares it's going to be 'the trip of a lifetime!' Before the first episode aired, documentary series *Doctor Who Confidential* ran a half hour programme examining the series' past while interviewing Davies, Tranter, Gardner, Collins, director Eros Lyn and the stars, and showing behind-the-scenes footage. The documentary was narrated by David Tennant.

- Every episode was complemented by its own edition of *Doctor Who Confidential*, narrated by Anthony Head and broadcast on BBC Three.

- *Doctor Who* won numerous accolades from the National Television Awards and BAFTA. The spotlight fell on Russell T Davies, Christopher Eccleston and Billie Piper in particular. Later, the show would be recognised in the United States by the science fiction Hugo Awards.

- Readers of *Doctor Who Magazine* voted Steven Moffat's *The Empty Child* as the best story of the season, and Christopher Eccleston topped Tom Baker in the Favourite Doctor category.

- When the second season was commissioned, most involved signed up to continue. One who didn't was actor Christopher Eccleston, who felt that the character's nuances and idiosyncrasies were becoming repetitive and predictable. It is also alleged that he had disagreements with directors and was becoming increasingly unhappy. However, he is on record as stating that he is proud to have made a series aimed at families. Once they knew Eccleston wouldn't be renewing his contract, Russell T Davies and Julie Gardner met with David Tennant, who had starred in Davies' BBC version of *Casanova* to see how he felt about becoming the next Doctor. Tennant was a lifelong devotee of *Doctor Who*. Julie Gardner reported that, 'We had him at "Hello".'

CHAPTER 12

THE DOCTOR
As played by
David Tennant

2005-2010

The Tenth Doctor is glad to be alive. Following his regeneration, he loves life, and the human race especially. Dressed in a pinstriped suit, white training shoes and a trench coat, this Doctor is a stark contrast to his previous self. What sounded to the untrained ear as a north England accent is now a generic south England dialect. The emotional effects of the Time War are less evident. The Doctor celebrates life in all its varieties.

Wearing his heart on his sleeve, the Doctor can be like an excitable child when encountering new things, and passionate when confronted with injustice. He will marvel at a creature that inspired legends about the Devil, and fall in love with a French monarch, only to have his heart broken. It will be broken again when his friendship with Rose is forced to end.

The Doctor cries over the apparent death of his arch-enemy, stymies a regeneration to retain the same form, reduces a companion to an ignorant 'chav' in order to save her life, and gives his own life to save an old man who's become like a father figure to him.

Who is the Doctor?

Resolutely stating that he is nine hundred and three in *Voyage of the Damned*, the question of the Doctor's real age is called to mind once more. And while the angst of being the Time War's sole survivor has subsided, he does recall Gallifrey's beauty with a tear in his eye.

When forced to part company with Rose, the Doctor comes as close as ever to actually saying 'I love you.' Perhaps his more youthful appearance has awakened a sense of romance in him. We certainly have never seen the Doctor so emotionally unguarded before. When appearing at different stages of Reinette de Pompadour's life, he is spellbound, and for the first time we witness the Doctor falling in love. She is able to see into his soul and describes him as her 'lonely angel'. Another first is seeing the Doctor grief stricken when he arrives after she has died.

To avoid detection by the Family of Blood, the Doctor uses the Chameleon Arch to create a non-Time Lord pseudo-personality–Dr John Smith–and hides in 1913 England as a teacher at a public school. There, John Smith falls in love with Joan Redfern, but when the Family of Blood is vanquished he turns himself back into the Doctor and has no choice but to leave her. Acquiring the fob watch containing the Doctor's memories and identity, young Timothy Latimer describes the Time Lord as 'like fire and ice and rage. He's like the night and the storm in the heart of the sun. He's ancient and forever. He burns at the centre of time and can see the turn of the universe.'

Upon learning that his arch-enemy The Master survived the Time War, the Doctor is both horrified to know the evil genius is at large and relieved to find out he isn't the last of the Time Lords after all.

When fatally wounded by a Dalek, the Doctor is consumed by the regeneration process. But as he cannot afford to endure post-regeneration confusion at a time of pandemic disaster, he directs the energy into his disembodied hand, thus healing himself but not transforming into a new incarnation. The cells in the hand grow a duplicate Doctor, who only has one heart and is completely human.

The Doctor speaks of the Shadow Proclamation and the Medusa Cascade and implies that he was directly involved in the final act of the Time War. It was he who banished Gallifrey into another dimension and walled it off with a time lock.

Sick of seeing good people suffer and die in the name of valour, the Doctor arrogantly declares himself 'Time Lord Victorious' and changes an established historical event to save someone's life. But when she commits suicide to correct the path of history, the Doctor knows he has overstepped the mark.

A woman with psychic abilities tells him a great darkness will soon descend upon him. It will be the worst of times. His present life will be forfeit when someone 'knocks four times' ...

Try these on DVD!

These stories are available as 'vanilla' releases (three episodes per disc) or as part of series/season box sets.

The Christmas Invasion - The TARDIS crashes to Earth and the newly regenerated Doctor tumbles out. He collapses in front of Jackie and Mickey. While our hero recovers from the trauma of metamorphosis and renewal, his companions deal with the Sycorax, who are holding the human race to ransom by conditioning a third of the world's populace to go up to the roofs of buildings, ready to throw themselves off. Will the Doctor recover in time to save the day, and what will his new persona be like? This is the very first Christmas special in the series' entire history, and is a most engaging and enjoyable romp.

In *New Earth* the Doctor and Rose travel five billion and twenty-three years into the future to visit Earth's replacement. At a hospital centre they encounter the female cat nuns (the Sisters of Plentitude) and discover the truth behind their miraculous cures. Unfortunately, they also encounter the Lady Cassandra again ...

If by now you've watched a good deal of *Doctor Who*, you will love *School Reunion*. An alien race of Krillitanes have taken over a school and are brainwashing the kids. Investigative reporter Sarah Jane Smith is hot on the case. When the Doctor and Rose arrive to uncover the truth (with the Doctor posing as a supply teacher), they summon the help of Rose's long-suffering boyfriend Mickey. The Doctor is thrilled to be reunited with Sarah and is overjoyed to see K9 again. But Sarah wants to know why he never came back to see her, and Rose is faced with stark reality–her relationship with the Doctor isn't unique, she is one of many.

The Girl in the Fireplace sees the Doctor, Rose and Mickey arrive on an abandoned spaceship in the far future. A dimensional doorway opens onto a fireplace of eighteenth-century France and the bedroom of a little girl. She is being attacked by clockwork droids. A few minutes later the Doctor goes through the doorway again, only to find that time has moved on and the girl is now a woman; in fact she is royalty–she is Madame de Pompadour. This adventure is the very first true *Doctor Who* love story. It will break your heart.

Arriving on an alternate Earth in the two-part *The Age of Steel/Rise of the Cybermen*, the Doctor, Rose and Mickey encounter John Lumic and his cyborg creations, the Cybermen. Rose gets the shock of her life when she finds that in this world her father never died and her parents are still married, and Mickey has an emotional reunion with his grandma. Meanwhile, Battersea Power Station has been converted into a processing plant where London's waifs and strays are being turned into an army of Cybermen.

The Impossible Planet/The Satan Pit - At a distant outpost, a skeleton crew man a spacecraft orbiting the planet Krop Tor. The crew are served by a slave race called the Ood. But the Ood are being channelled by something ancient and evil down on the planet. As the crew are picked off one by one, the Doctor goes down to the planet and deep into the cavern, where he finds what appears to be the Devil ...

The Runaway Bride - In this fun Christmas special, the Doctor has little time to mourn the loss of Rose, as a woman dressed in a bridal gown and veil appears in the TARDIS. The woman is called Donna Noble and she has attitude. Meanwhile, a arachnoid creature, the Empress of the Racnoss, is planning to release itself and wreak havoc on the world. Donna not only has to come to terms with the reality of alien life, but in the end has to temper the Doctor's ruthless streak. He shouldn't travel alone, she concludes.

The Tenth Doctor's second season kicks off with *Smith and Jones*. The Doctor is investigating strange goings-on at a hospital. Medical student Martha Jones is also on the case. When the entire hospital building is transferred to the moon, they are in no doubt that the alien presence intends to harvest all of the occupants. And then come the Judoon, an intergalactic police force who intend to sterilise the situation.

Human Nature/The Family of Blood - The Doctor must use the Chameleon Arch to avoid detection by the Family of Blood. He turns himself into an ordinary human being–Dr John Smith–and teaches at a boys' school in 1913. John Smith has no idea who he really is, or that his maid Martha is his time-travelling companion. The Family track the Time Lord to the area and use scarecrows to attack the school. Martha really needs the Doctor back, but John Smith has fallen in love with Joan Redfern. The Doctor's true self is locked up in a device disguised as a pocket watch. Martha must get him to open it.

Blink - Sally Sparrow and her friend Kathy Nightingale go to investigate a derelict house after receiving a mysterious message. Statues in the garden seem to change poise and even location. Kathy is touched by one of them and is sent back in time to Hull in the 1920s, where she must live out the rest of her life. She writes a message that Sally Sparrow will find in the future. Meanwhile, Kathy's brother Larry has found a concealed message from a man called the Doctor on a host of DVDs. The Doctor says the Weeping Angels—the statues—are living beings which feed off time energy. Sally and Larry must go back to the house but avoid being touched by the Angels. The creatures can only move when they aren't being observed–so the couple mustn't take their eyes off them for a second, they mustn't even blink. This is by far one of the spookiest adventures in *Doctor Who*'s entire history.

In the three-part *Utopia//The Sound of Drums/Last of the Time Lords*, the Doctor and Martha are confronted by the time anomaly that is Captain Jack Harkness. In an attempt to shake him off, the TARDIS travels far into the future to a planet where the last humans are struggling to survive. A scientist called Professor Yana is hoping to transport the survivors to a new world, the mythical Utopia. But upon meeting the Doctor, the old man is deeply troubled. He experiences voices from the past, as though he and the Doctor are somehow already acquainted. The sight of the TARDIS makes matters worse for him. When the Doctor, Martha and Jack go to Earth, the Doctor's arch-enemy the Master has assumed the role of Harold Saxon, prime minister of Great Britain. But what of the survivors of Earth's future who were sent to Utopia?

In Tennant's third season story *The Fires of Pompeii*, the Doctor has been reunited with Donna Noble and the pair arrive in Pompeii the day before Mount Vesuvius erupts. The destruction of Pompeii is a fixed point in time, so the Doctor determines to let history run its course. But it isn't as simple as that, as an alien presence is manipulating events, and Donna has bonded with one particular family. Can't the Doctor save them at least?

Planet of the Ood - the Doctor and Donna land on the home world of the Ood. The Doctor finds a corrupt business initiative bent on exploiting the creatures. Without being preachy, this story is a fine and moving consideration of the issue of slavery.

Silence in the Library/Forest of the Dead - The Doctor and Donna explore the planet-sized book repository—the Library. A young girl is watching events on television in her bedroom. Who is she and where is she? Then a team of archaeologists turn up, led by one Professor River Song. She is astounded when she realises she's dealing with the Doctor. She knows him of old and even hints at their possibly being married. Consulting an oblong blue book, she checks which events they've shared together to date as their paths have crossed, only to realise that none of it has actually happened to the Doctor yet. 'You're so young,' she says (referring to his tenth incarnation, not the fact that he looks young). But this mystery will have to wait, because living shadows are picking off her team one by one. Then they get Donna ...

Midnight - With Donna resting and treating herself at an intergalactic health spa, the Doctor takes a trip on a shuttle to see a waterfall made of sapphires. Something has possessed a passenger named Sky Silvestry and repeats everything the Doctor says, driving him and the other passengers to distraction. With a small cast, a clever script and excellent performances from David Tennant and guest star Lesley Sharp, this is a tense and engaging psychological drama.

In *Turn Left*, Donna's timeline is split into two possibilities. In one, she turns right at a road junction and her life unfolds in a way that means she never met the Doctor. But someone is trying to contact her–a young woman called Rose–and there's this phrase, 'Bad Wolf' ...

The Stolen Earth/Journey's End - The Earth and several other planets from around the universe have been transported across the vast regions of space to one location. The Daleks are involved and the Doctor is shocked to find that their creator Davros, whom he'd assumed was long since dead after the Time War, is alive and well. What do all the planets have in common, and why have they been gathered together? Martha, Captain Jack, UNIT, former prime minister Harriet Jones and Sarah Jane Smith join forces to aid the Time Lord. But the Doctor has been reunited with Rose. His joy is short-lived when he is shot by a Dalek and the regeneration process is triggered ...

The Next Doctor is the Christmas episode of 2008 and the first of the four specials leading up to David Tennant's departure (there was no regular television series in 2009). The Doctor is travelling alone again. He arrives in London on Christmas Eve 1851 and is astonished to find another man called the Doctor, who travels with a faithful companion named Rosita. Could this be the Doctor's next incarnation? The two gentlemen must join forces to battle Cybermen that have fallen through time and are planning on building a Cyber King.

Planet of the Dead is the Easter 2009 special and was described by Russell T Davies as the Tenth Doctor's last hurrah. It is a fun romp involving an aristocratic cat burglar named Lady Christina de Souza, a double-decker bus stranded in an alien desert, and a swarm of stingray-like aliens intent on reaching Earth. The Doctor is warned by a lady with clairvoyant capabilities that she sees dark times ahead for him, and a cryptic clue–'He will knock four times'.

The Waters of Mars was written by Russell T Davies and Phil Ford, the first co-authorship of the twenty-first century series. The Doctor arrives at a base on Mars to find that something in the water is turning members of the skeleton crew into zombies. With the odds stacked against him, the Doctor declares himself Time Lord Victorious–as the only remaining Gallifreyan he is going to act as a god and change history. Has he finally gone too far?

The End of Time parts one and two - The Doctor is disturbed by his recent actions on Mars and is all too aware that the prophecy 'He will knock four times' is due to be fulfilled. But what does it mean–his death? He is summoned by the Ood to hear even more disturbing news: the Master has succeeded in having himself resurrected, albeit in an incomplete state, and something else is set to return–Gallifrey. When the Master uses the Immortality Gate to turn almost every human being on Earth into a copy of himself, little does he realise that he is being manipulated by Lord Rassilon and the High Council of Time Lords. They endeavour to use him to gain entry to the real universe. The Doctor must stop them, no matter the cost.

Miscellany

- David Tennant uttered his first words as the Doctor at the end of Christopher Eccleston's last episode *The Parting of the Ways* in June 2005. A short scene in which the new Doctor struggles to stabilise and Rose asks if he can change back featured in that year's *Children in Need* charity fundraising programme. The scene finished with the Doctor losing control of the TARDIS. This would lead directly into the beginning of *The Christmas Invasion*, broadcast on Christmas Day.
- Elisabeth Sladen was delighted to return to the role of

Sarah Jane Smith for *School Reunion*. John Leeson supplied the voice of K9 once again. The success of the episode led to the commissioning of the Children's BBC series *The Sarah Jane Adventures*, in which Sarah was joined by K9 as well as a computer called Mr Smith, a genetically engineered boy named Luke (whom she adopts as her son) and his friends from the local school. The series proved to be a big hit.

- The acronym UNIT was changed from United Nations Intelligence Taskforce to Unified Intelligence Taskforce.

- While episodes of *Doctor Who* were being passed around the various production departments of the BBC, to avoid detection by the press, they were labelled 'Torchwood' (an anagram of 'Doctor Who'). Russell T Davies was keen to make an adult spin-off series from the show and so began referencing the phrase Torchwood as a secret government organisation that made use of alien technology that it had seized. The first reference was in *The Christmas Invasion*. All of this was designed to build interest in the new series *Torchwood*. Set in modern-day Cardiff, the series shows the Torchwood organisation operating in a base situated on the time rift mentioned in the previous year's *The Unquiet Dead* and *Boomtown*. When Captain Jack becomes involved, he assumes control of the centre. The series was broadcast after the watershed on BBC Three. It was an adult drama and so contained swearing and sexual references. The BBC received complaints from concerned parents, since *Torchwood* had been heavily promoted in episodes of *Doctor Who*–a family drama watched by young children. This led to an edited version of the programme being shown at a pre-watershed time on BBC Two.

- In *The Christmas Invasion*, the newly regenerated Doctor engages the Sycorax leader in a sword fight. The Doctor's right hand is severed and falls from the Sycorax spaceship down into the city of London below. Since the Doctor's body is still regenerating, it grows a replacement hand. The detached hand is later discovered by Captain Jack in the spin-off series *Torchwood*, who then returns it to the Doctor in the *Doctor Who* story *Utopia*. Later, the hand is grown into a 'meta-crisis' clone of the Doctor, but with only one heart and one life. He lives out the rest of his days on an alternate Earth.

- The two-part *The Age of Steel/Rise of the Cybermen* by Tom Macrae was based on a Big Finish audio drama by Marc Platt entitled *Spare Parts*. This starred Peter Davison as the Fifth Doctor and Sarah Sutton as Nyssa, who witness the gradual birth of the Cybermen on Mondas. Audio producer Gary Russell told Marc Platt there should be no 'Cyber Davros'–a creator figure. The development of the Cybermen as outlined by writers Gerry Davis and Kit Pedler in the 1960s was that the characters became like that over time as they replaced vital organs with cybernetics, eventually replacing the brain with computers. However, Tom Macrae's TV version saw Roger Lloyd Pack playing John Lumic, an insane genius and businessman in an alternate reality who designs and builds the Cybermen on Earth. At the time of publication, the classic series Mondas-originated Cybermen have never made an appearance in the revived show.

- The two-part *Human Nature/Family of Blood* was adapted from Virgin Publishing's *Doctor Who– The New Adventures* novel *Human Nature* by its author Paul Cornell. In the book, it is the Seventh Doctor who turns himself into John Smith so that the Aubertide (rather than the Family of Blood) cannot trace him, and it is his companion Bernice (created for the book range) who becomes his maid. The device that turns him back into the Doctor was disguised as cricket ball, but for the TV version this was changed to a pocket watch so the same plot device could be reused later. To add an extra strand of action, Russell T Davies requested that Cornell have the Family of Blood animate scarecrows and use them as an army of zombies.

- In the first two of the Russell T Davies-produced seasons, scriptwriter Steven Moffat won the Best Writer accolade in *Doctor Who Magazine* each time, for *The Empty Child* and *The Girl in the Fireplace*. Rumour has it that for the third season Davies assigned Moffat the 'Doctor-lite' story (an episode in which the Doctor and companion hardly feature so that David Tennant and his co-star can film two stories at the same time) to ensure that he wouldn't win the category again. Moffat left writing his script to the eleventh hour, and in desperation looked to the children's game Statues (or Grandmother's

Footsteps) for inspiration. What he came up with was the concept of the Weeping Angels and the episode *Blink*. Both topped their respective categories in the *DWM* poll for that season. The Weeping Angels beat the Daleks in popularity and *Blink* is constantly listed as one of the best stories ever.

* Freema Agyeman made *Doctor Who* history as the first black female travelling companion of the Doctor, Martha Jones.

* The Face of Boe, a character that first appears in the Ninth Doctor adventure *The End of the World*, returns two more times in the Tenth Doctor's era, each time fleetingly, to utter cryptic prophecies about the Time Lord's near future.

* The casting of comedienne and actress Catherine Tate as Donna Noble in *The Runaway Bride* proved so successful that Russell T Davies chose to bring back the character for Tennant's final full season. Popular actor Bernard Cribbins (who had starred alongside Peter Cushing's Dr. Who in the 1966 movie *Daleks–Invasion Earth 2150 AD*) made a cameo appearance in *Voyage of the Damned*. Davies decided Cribbins would be Donna's granddad. He featured in the final season and played a pivotal role in the Tenth Doctor's last episode.

* Peter Davison reprised his role of the Fifth Doctor and met David Tennant as the current incarnation in the skit *Time Crash* as part of the BBC's 2007 fundraising event *Children in Need*.
* Pop star and actress Kylie Minogue guest starred as

Astrid Peth in the 2007 Christmas special *Voyage of the Damned*.

- The Doctor's arch-enemy the Master made his first reappearance in the revived series in the 2007 episode *Utopia*. Having been resurrected by Time itself during the Time War, it would appear the character now has a new cycle of regenerations. In *Utopia*, Derek Jacobi plays the Doctor's nemesis before regenerating into John Simm.

- By the time he began writing *Silence in the Library*, Steven Moffat knew he was going to be Russell T Davies' successor as Head Writer and Executive Producer. A few days before beginning the script, he asked David Tennant for a definite decision as to whether he would continue into his era as the Doctor. Moffat introduced the character of Professor River Song, who, it seemed, had been married to the Doctor in her past, yet none of this had happened to the Doctor–it was still in his future. Moffat got the idea from reading Audrey Niffenegger's novel *The Time Traveller's Wife*.

- For the first time in *Doctor Who* history, a special elite of Daleks is devised; they are called the Cult of Skaro. Made up of four individual Daleks programmed to think and reason as their enemies do, these creatures have names: Dalek Sec, Dalek Thay, Dalek Caan and Dalek Jast. In *Daleks in Manhattan*, Dalek Sec chooses to be turned into a human, but his plan backfires when he begins to truly reason as a human and sees the Daleks for what they are.

In *The Stolen Earth*, the last of the Cult to survive, Dalek Caan, has looked into the Time Vortex and gone insane. He revels in his ability to make cryptic prophecies about the future of the Daleks and the Doctor.

- In *The End of Time*, the President of the High Council of Time Lords, Lord Rassilon, is played by ex-James Bond, Timothy Dalton. Rassilon states that during the Time War, Time Lords were resurrected by Time itself over and over so that they could continue to fight. Presumably, both he and the Master were among these.

- Throughout David Tennant's time as the Doctor, both he and the series won numerous prestigious awards. At the National Television Awards ceremony, Tennant gratefully accepted his award for Outstanding Drama Performance and then shocked the audience by announcing that he would only be making four special episodes in 2009 before departing the role. In a BBC News announcement about the actor's decision to leave, newsreader George Alagiah declared David Tennant to be the most popular Doctor Who ever.

CHAPTER 13

THE DOCTOR
As played by
Matt Smith

2010-13

The Eleventh Doctor is handsome and younger in appearance than any of his predecessors. A very dapper incarnation, he sports a bow tie (proudly declaring that 'Bow ties are cool!') with a stylish tweed jacket or frock coat and occasionally a fez! Shortly after the regeneration, the eccentric nature of this Doctor becomes clear when he displays an inexplicable desire to eat fish fingers and custard, and we later learn he is partial to Jammie Dodger biscuits. He also displays a hitherto unseen ability to play football. Despite this lighter side, he is all too aware that he has just one more regeneration before his life cycle is up ...

This Doctor develops a particularly close relationship with his first companion, Amelia Pond. Due to the wonders of time travel, he first meets Amy when she is a little girl before encountering her again as a young woman, and she comes to regard him as her 'raggedy man'. When Amy later tries to seduce the Doctor, he is simply not interested–despite his human appearance, it is clear that the Doctor is still very much an alien! When it is time for the Doctor to regenerate again, an image of Amy appears before him, suggesting that she has been his most precious companion ...

Who is the Doctor?

The personality of the Eleventh Doctor is shaped by his relationships with his friends–and by cataclysmic events on a universal scale.

The newly regenerated Doctor encounters the seven-year-old Amelia Pond and then, returning five minutes later from his perspective, meets her again when she is twelve years older. There is a crack in the wall of

Amy's bedroom which the Doctor realises is a crack in time and space. He later discovers that the crack is due to an explosion in time and that anything falling into it will cease to exist. Admitting he is lonely, the Time Lord invites Amy to join him on his travels in the TARDIS. The Doctor once again meets Professor River Song, and it is clear that although it is only his second encounter with her, she has met him many times before in her time stream, as they are travelling through time in opposite directions.

Later, the Doctor, Amy and Amy's fiancé Rory encounter a pseudo-incarnation of the Doctor who turns out to be a manifestation of the Time Lord's dark side and self-loathing.

Following an encounter with the Silurians, Rory is killed and absorbed into another crack, meaning he will be erased from history, and the Doctor pulls what appears to be a piece of the TARDIS from the crack.

River summons the Doctor and Amy to Stonehenge in 102 AD. Under the henge is a fabled prison called the Pandorica, and it transpires that an alliance of the Doctor's greatest enemies have come together to try to imprison him to prevent the cracks in time that will destroy the universe. It is in fact the explosion of the TARDIS that causes the universe to end, but the Doctor uses time travel to reboot the universe, as a consequence of which Rory is resurrected and he and Amy are married. The Doctor himself is temporarily erased from history but brought back by Amy's memories of him.

In Utah, USA, Amy, Rory and River appear to witness the death of the Doctor at the hands of a mysterious figure in a spacesuit. River turns out to be Melody Pond, daughter of Amy and Rory, and as she was conceived in the time vortex, she is able to regenerate like the Doctor, although she ultimately sacrifices her remaining regenerations to save the Doctor's life. It is also revealed that River was the girl in the spacesuit—why does she want to kill the Time Lord, and can she be prevented from doing so? And why do the mysterious religious order called the Silence have such an interest in the Doctor's ultimate destiny?

After Amy and Rory are trapped in the past by the evil Weeping Angels, the Doctor meets a girl called Clara Oswald, who appears to have led multiple lives and who for some reason the TARDIS appears not to like! It transpires that there are echoes of Clara spread throughout time, saving the Doctor at various points during his many lives.

Ultimately, the Doctor has to confront the consequences of his decision to destroy Gallifrey during the Time War, and with two of his past incarnations he takes radical action to put things right. Their solution is to hide Gallifrey in a pocket dimension, but when the Time Lords try to break back through via another crack in time located on the planet Trenzalore, the Doctor keeps vigil to stop them returning and prevent another Time War erupting. The Time Lords want him to answer the question 'Doctor who?' so that he will name himself and prove who he is, showing them it is safe to return, but he is unprepared to do this. Aware that Trenzalore is the location of his future grave and therefore his final resting place, the Doctor is resigned to dying there, when Clara asks the Time Lords for help in extending his regenerative cycle ...

Try these on DVD!

Like the David Tennant episodes, Matt Smith's stories can be bought in a variety of formats.

The Eleventh Hour - With the Doctor newly regenerated, the TARDIS makes a crash-landing on Earth in the village of Leadworth. After adopting Amy Pond as his new companion, the Doctor receives a psychic message from a race called the Atraxi, stating that 'Prisoner Zero has escaped.' Prisoner Zero is a shape-shifting alien which can adopt the appearance of anything from a man with a dog on a leash to Amy herself! The Atraxi are galactic police and if Prisoner Zero is not returned to them, they will destroy the Earth!

The two-part *The Time of Angels/Flesh and Stone* features the return of the popular but scary Weeping Angels! The Doctor and Amy arrive at a museum in the future and find a message from River Song. The message leads them to a spaceship where they rescue River, but in the hold of the ship, which crashes, is one of the sinister Weeping Angels previously encountered by the Tenth Doctor. They'll need to stop the angel before radiation from the ship makes it too powerful, because there's a nearby human colony to protect ...

A bizarre turn of events in *Amy's Choice* sees the Doctor, Amy and Rory fall asleep in the TARDIS and then wake up in Leadworth. Who is the strange man taunting them? Which reality is the true one? If Amy makes the wrong choice, the three friends will die.

In the two-part *The Hungry Earth/Cold Blood*, the TARDIS arrives in Wales in the year 2020. A drilling operation results in unusual holes appearing in the ground and the disappearance of individuals. The Doctor discovers that a Silurian colony is hibernating directly beneath them. When a Silurian woman named Alaya is held captive, it transpires she hopes to spark a war between her race and the humans and reclaim planet Earth. As in the Third Doctor adventure *Doctor Who and the Silurians*, the Doctor hopes to be the mediator of peace. But how can he succeed when both sides are suspicious, paranoid and mistrusting of the other?

Vincent and the Doctor sees the Doctor cross paths with the famous artist Vincent Van Gogh. After seeing an alien figure in a window in one of Van Gogh's paintings, the Doctor and Amy travel to Provence to meet the artist. They discover that the area is being terrorised by an invisible creature called the Krafayis, which only Van Gogh can see. Van Gogh appears to have little in the way of self-worth and it's up to the Doctor to convince him that he will become not only a great artist, but one of the greatest men of all time.

In *The Lodger*, the TARDIS materialises in present-day Colchester. When the Doctor steps out, the ship immediately dematerialises, taking Amy with it. Meanwhile, a young man named Craig and his flatmate Sophie seem to be the focus of whatever is 'disturbing' the TARDIS. Trying to masquerade as a normal human being, the Doctor becomes Craig's lodger in order to investigate the mysterious locked door on the building's second storey. An alien presence in that upper room is luring people off the street and killing them. But who or what is in that room? Part mystery, part comedy, this standalone adventure shows off the acting talent of star Matt Smith.

The Doctor's Wife - The Doctor believes that his own race is entirely extinct, so he is surprised to receive a distress call which appears to be from a Time Lord. However, the call is in fact a trick to lure him to an asteroid occupied by strange inhabitants called Uncle and Auntie, an Ood called Nephew and a strange young woman called Idris. The asteroid is actually a sentient entity called House, which is able to possess technology and Uncle and Auntie are made up of body parts from other beings, including Time Lords! But what are the strange white message cubes that the Doctor finds stored in a cabinet? And who is Idris, and how is she connected to the Doctor's TARDIS?

The Girl Who Waited is a great opportunity for actress Karen Gillan to shine as the Doctor's companion Amy. The Doctor, Amy and Rory go to the planet Apalapucia for a holiday, but the planet is suffering from a terrible plague. The TARDIS has materialised in a stark white room with an exit and two buttons labelled 'Green Anchor' and 'Red Waterfall'. The Doctor and Rory press the green button and step into another room, but Amy follows later and presses the red one. Amy also steps into a room, but the Doctor and Rory are not there and it transpires she has passed into a faster time stream. When they finally find her, they have remained the same age but she is thirty-six years older and understandably bitter. The Doctor is faced with the moral dilemma of whether he can rescue both the young and the old Amy, an action which will cause a time paradox.

A Town Called Mercy is set in the American Wild West, where a cyborg 'Gunslinger' is refusing to allow anyone in or out of the town. The Doctor realises that the man being held in jail is of alien origin and the Gunslinger wants revenge against those who created him.

The Power of Three picks up the tale of Amy and Rory, the married couple now having spent some time away from the Doctor. The Time Lord re-enters their lives when millions of small black cubes appear all around the world over night. At first they seem like a peculiar natural occurrence, but after a while it is evident that something or someone has sent them. The tension mounts as each cube begins a countdown cycle–but a countdown to what?

The Snowmen sees the return of the Great Intelligence, an enemy from the Troughton era. Previously, the Intelligence had controlled the robot Yeti, but in this story it's living snowmen who are threatening the Doctor! The story takes place in the Victorian era, and the Snowmen need human DNA in ice crystal form to take over the human race. Can the Doctor stop them?

Hide is a nice, self-contained haunted house-style story! Arriving in the 1970s, the Doctor and Clara visit what appears to be a haunted mansion. The so-called resident 'ghost' is in fact a time traveller from the future trapped in a pocket universe. Unable to use the TARDIS, the Doctor needs to find another way to help the time traveller.

Cold War - Another Troughton-era foe returns in a very traditional and exciting episode. The Doctor and Clara arrive on a Russian submarine in the year 1983. The submarine has been transporting a creature encased in ice, which is in fact one of the reptilian Ice Warriors from Mars. Despite attempts to restrain it, the Ice Warrior escapes and goes on the rampage, and if that were not enough to deal with, the Time Lord and his companion have to convince the crew that they are not Western spies–and try to avoid World War Three!

In *The Name of the Doctor*, the Doctor's friends Madame Vastra (a Silurian), her maid Jenny Flint, Sontaran Commander Strax, River Song and Clara meet in a bizarre dream realm. Vastra has been given information about the Doctor and space/time coordinates for the planet Trenzalore. When creepy faceless humanoids called Whisper Men attack Vastra, Flint and Strax, the Doctor decides he must visit Trenzalore to rescue them, even though it is the location of his own grave and therefore very dangerous for him to visit. There, he once again encounters the Great Intelligence, and Clara enters the Doctor's personal timeline, meeting his past incarnations. This story leads nicely into ...

The Day of the Doctor - a stunning episode for the fiftieth anniversary, this celebratory special sees the return of the Tenth Doctor and another incarnation we'd previously known nothing about–the War Doctor! The War Doctor falls between the Time Lord's Ninth and Tenth incarnations but does not call himself the Doctor. He is the one who fought in the Time War, and the other Doctors must help him decide if destroying the Daleks

178

and Time Lords really is the way to bring the war to an end. Also in this amazing story, the Tenth Doctor gets himself into trouble when he encounters the Zygons, and the Eleventh incarnation meets a familiar face at the National Art Gallery in London …

Miscellany

- New *Doctor Who* Executive Producer Steven Moffat had intended casting an actor in his forties for the role of the Eleventh Doctor, but ultimately cast Matt Smith, who at twenty-six was the youngest actor ever to play the part. Smith had also auditioned for the part of Dr Watson in Moffat's other hit series, *Sherlock*, but Moffat felt him too eccentric for the role. When it came to the Doctor, however, Smith was felt to be ideal.

- *The Eleventh Hour* saw several changes for the programme. There was a new title sequence, logo, theme arrangement (again composed by Murray Gold), TARDIS exterior and interior and a new version of the sonic screwdriver. The 2011 Christmas special, *The Snowmen*, would utilise yet another new version of the title sequence, this time featuring the Doctor's face in the opening credits for the first time since Sylvester McCoy's last season in 1989.

- Karen Gillan, who played companion Amy Pond, had previously appeared in the David Tennant episode *The Fires of Pompeii*. Gillan's cousin Caitlin Blackwood played the seven-year-old version of Amy.

- *Victory of the Daleks* saw the introduction of new, larger and more colourful Daleks called the Paradigm Daleks, which were partly inspired by the Daleks seen in the 1960s Peter Cushing *Dr. Who* movies. Not everyone liked them, with some observers comparing them to the children's television characters the Teletubbies! Also in this story, we discover that the Doctor is friends with British wartime Prime Minister Winston Churchill.

- *Vincent and the Doctor* was written by Richard Curtis, one of Britain's most successful comedy screen writers, who had been behind such hits as the BBC's *Blackadder* and the feature film *Four Weddings and a Funeral*. He had also been Executive Producer of *Doctor Who and the Curse of Fatal Death*, a special Comic Relief episode of *Doctor Who* made in 1999 and starring Rowan Atkinson as the Doctor. *Vincent and the Doctor* co-starred successful British actor Bill Nighy, who himself had once been rumoured to be playing the Doctor.

- The episode *The Pandorica Opens* featured the largest assembly of monsters ever seen in *Doctor Who*– Daleks, Cybermen, Sontarans, Autons, Silurians and Sycorax were amongst the creatures who united to form an alliance against the Doctor.

- The 2010 Christmas special, *A Christmas Carol,* featured the acting debut of Welsh singer Katherine Jenkins, who played Abigail. As the script called for Abigail to sing, Jenkins was a natural choice, but she admitted that she was nervous about taking on the role due to her lack of acting experience.

- Unusually, Smith's second season was shown in two parts, with episodes 1 to 7 broadcast from April to June 2011, and the final six episodes from August to October.

- The opening story of Matt Smith's second season, comprising the episodes *The Impossible Astronaut/ The Day of the Moon,* was the first *Doctor Who* story to utilise principal photography footage filmed in the United States (second unit establishing shots having been filmed in New York for the David Tennant episode *Daleks in Manhattan*).

- The new monsters known collectively as The Silence, which debuted in *The Impossible Astronaut*, were intended to be one of the scariest ever villains in *Doctor Who*. Their faces were based on Edvard Munch's famous 1893 expressionist painting *The Scream.*

- In Matt Smith's second season episode *A Good Man Goes to War*, Steven Moffat introduced what has been sometimes called the Paternoster Gang, a trio of semi-regular characters. The Doctor calls in old favours from a Silurian named Vastra and her human maid Jenny, and a Sontaran 'nurse' called Strax. He wants them, along with others, to help him rescue Amy. Later, in *The Snowmen*, Madame Vastra, Jenny and Strax are living in nineteenth-century London, where they hope to lure the Doctor out of retirement. They return again in *The Crimson Horror*, the Eleventh Doctor's finale *The Time of the Doctor* and aid the Twelfth Doctor after his regeneration in *Deep Breath*.

- The voice of the malevolent entity known as House in *The Doctor's Wife* was provided by famous British actor Michael Sheen, who is well known for playing real-life people such as former British Prime Minister Tony Blair and Sir David Frost in movies. Another acting legend, Sir Ian McKellen, played the voice of the Great Intelligence in *The Snowmen*.

- *The Wedding of River Song* brings the story of one of the Doctor's oldest allies, Brigadier Alistair Gordon Lethbridge-Stewart, to a close when the Doctor is told on the telephone that his old friend has died peacefully in a nursing home. Actor Nicholas Courtney, who played the Brigadier, passed away in 2011.

- The BBC boasted that the episode *Asylum of the Daleks* would feature 'every Dalek ever'. Whilst this proved to be something of an exaggeration, a wide variety of Dalek designs did appear, including the Special Weapons Dalek which had featured in the Sylvester McCoy story *Remembrance of the Daleks*. Several Daleks were sourced from old exhibitions and fans of the series. One of the Daleks used was owned by former *Doctor Who* showrunner Russell T Davies.

- In his final season, the Eleventh Doctor travels with Clara Oswald, whom he dubs the Impossible Girl. On two previous occasions, he had encountered young ladies of similar likeness (Oswin Oswald in *Asylum of the Daleks* and Clara Oswin Oswald in *The Snowmen*), both of whom perished while aiding him. The Doctor is determined to discover what links the three women through time.

- Actor David Warner, who had appeared in such science fiction mainstays as *Tron*, two *Star Trek* films, *Planet of the Apes* and some *Doctor Who* audio stories, finally got his chance to appear in televised *Doctor Who* in *Cold War*.

- The Eleventh Doctor's final story, *The Time of the Doctor,* saw the return of some of the scariest monsters from his era–the Daleks, Cybermen, Sontarans, Weeping Angels and the Silence all make an appearance. This was the eight-hundredth episode of *Doctor Who* to be broadcast.

- Although Matt Smith was the eleventh incarnation of the famous Time Lord, we learn in *The Time of the Doctor* that the Doctor had used up all thirteen of his lives. That's because the War Doctor, played by John Hurt, counts as a regeneration, and the Tenth Doctor aborted a regeneration so that he wouldn't change his appearance–the vanity!

CHAPTER 14

THE DOCTOR
As played by
Peter Capaldi

2013-?

The Twelfth Doctor is really the Fourteenth Doctor.

The War Doctor had been the Time Lord's ninth incarnation, although his later selves choose not to count him as such. The Tenth Doctor had regenerated twice, and on the first occasion kept the same face. So after his final life runs its course, the Doctor is facing certain death. Blessed at the crucial moment with a new cycle of regenerations, the Doctor regenerates into his twelfth persona–the first of a new line of thirteen. Or is it? Do the same rules apply second time around? Now all bets are off.

Who is the Doctor?

Appearing as a middle-aged man, the Doctor has little time for human niceties and social etiquette. He is less inclined to wear costumes and outfits, and most of his clothes are black. His coat has a red lining and he wears Dr Martens boots. Solving the mystery on his adventures is more important to him than reassuring people. If he can gain a vital piece of information from a dying man, he will forego words of comfort and press him for what he knows. The Doctor is haunted by the promise that Gallifrey will somehow return to normal space/time. He last encountered his own race when he despatched Lord Rassilon and The Master into that realm. But what became of the latter?

Try These Episodes!

These stories can be downloaded or can be seen in the Series Eight box set.

Into the Dalek - On the hospital-cum-military spaceship Aristotle, the Doctor and Clara help the crew investigate why the Dalek they are holding prisoner is malfunctioning–why it is being nice. Along with crew members Ross, Gretchen and Blue, they are miniaturised and injected into the Dalek through its eyepiece. What is causing the Dalek to contemplate beauty and consider the wonders of the universe? Why does it now hold life to be sacred? And what will happen when the Dalek is 'fixed'? The Doctor in his new persona appears to care little, and employs some unique methods to acquire the information he needs.

Listen - The dream all people experience at some point in their lives–hands coming out from under the bed and grabbing one's ankles. Why? The Doctor has been travelling alone and has formulated a theory–that every living being has an unseen constant companion. To test the theory, he recruits Clara and connects her to the TARDIS' telepathic circuits. But instead of thinking of her own experience, she ponders on her boyfriend Danny Pink. The TARDIS transports them to his childhood where the Doctor, Clara and young Danny encounter a monster apparently made from bed sheets and a red eiderdown. Is it real or in their minds? And where does the nightmare common to all living things originate? The Doctor is shocked to find it is much closer to home than he ever could have known.

Mummy On the Orient Express - As her relationship with Danny strengthens, Clara is reluctant to continue her travels with the Doctor, especially as he seems so much more ruthless and detached following his regeneration. She agrees to 'one last hurrah' and goes with him to the space train The Orient Express. The train and its passengers are all in period dress to complete the illusion. But some of the passengers are there for a specific purpose; they want to chance an encounter with the legendary supernatural entity known as The Foretold, a being that materialises as an embalmed mummy which can only be seen by its victim for ninety seconds prior to their death. The Doctor is forced to admit that this is why he too is visiting the train. Clara is not impressed. When the Mummy appears, the Doctor must ascertain from the victims—who can see what it's like—how it advances and how it reacts to pleas for mercy. But the Doctor and his fellow passengers are not the only ones intent on learning the truth about the legend. Who or what has gathered everyone together? And what really is The Foretold?

Flatline - Arriving in Bristol, the Doctor is shocked to find that the TARDIS exterior is shrinking. He and Clara can barely get through the door. He rushes back inside to try and stabilise the dimensions. Clara meets Rigsy, a young man doing community service wiping graffiti from a pedestrian tunnel. The backs of individuals have apparently been painted on the wall of the tunnel. Rigsy explains that they are a mural of recently missing people. But why did the unknown artist paint the backs of them? Meanwhile, the TARDIS has shrunk so much that Clara can carry it in her bag. The interior dimensions are unaffected, and the Doctor is able to pass his sonic screwdriver to her through the tiny door, along with his psychic paper and an earpiece so he can communicate with her. A race of two-dimensional beings the Doctor nicknames the Boneless are experimenting with the third dimension. Are they simply trying to understand our universe and the life in it, or is something more sinister going on?

Miscellany

- A lifelong *Doctor Who* enthusiast, young Peter Capaldi had been a member of the *Doctor Who* Fan Club in the 1970s and had sent prospective scripts to Pertwee era producer Barry Letts, who had offered encouragement to the young fan and invited him to visit the BBC studios. Capaldi also had a letter published in *Radio Times* in 1974, in which he congratulated the magazine on a *Doctor Who* special they had produced and expressed regret at the untimely death of actor Roger Delgado.

- After transmission of his initial season, Capaldi revealed that we could in fact have seen him much earlier as the Doctor—in 1996. The actor was asked to audition for the project that eventually became the Paul McGann TV movie, but he declined, feeling that he was not well-known enough. At the launch of his first series on DVD, he told fans: 'I didn't want the disappointment [after] going through all the palaver - jumping through hoops for something I would never get.'

- Shortly before being cast as the Twelfth Doctor, Capaldi appeared in the 2013 film *World War Z*, in which he was credited, bizarrely, as 'W.H.O. Doctor.

,

- Best known for playing Malcolm Tucker in the satirical BBC Two political comedy *The Thick of It*, Capaldi had also previously guest-starred in the David Tennant *Doctor Who* story *The Fires of Pompeii* (playing Caecilius) and the *Torchwood: Children of Earth* series as John Frobisher.

- The identity of the Twelfth Doctor was revealed to the world on a special live BBC programme called *Doctor Who Live: The Next Doctor* presented by Zoe Ball on 4 August 2013. Other names mooted for the role had included Ben Whishaw, Ben Daniels, David Harewood, Andrew Scott and Rory Kinnear, but in the days leading up to the announcement, Capaldi had become the bookies' favourite. Getting Capaldi to the studio was not easy, with the actor later revealing, 'There was a lot of cloak-and-dagger stuff... the BBC genuinely felt it had to maintain secrecy so I was taken to a car park, dropped off by one car and put in another car with a blanket over my head. For all I knew, because I couldn't see or hear anything, there might have been no one there and it could all have been a load of baloney.'

- Steven Moffat had asked fellow *Who* writer Mark Gatiss for his views on who should play the role: 'I asked my old friend Mark Gatiss to give me a list – he's brilliant at casting, Mark – and I asked him, could you make a list of people you think should be the Doctor, and right at the top of his list, with a space below him before the other names, was Peter Capaldi.'

- The title sequence for Capaldi's first season was based on a fan-made opening sequence by animator Billy Henshaw, featuring whirling cogs and spiralling clock faces which Moffat had seen on YouTube. Henshaw was asked to act as conceptual designer, working with the BBC Wales' VFX team to create the final version.

- The episode *Robot of Sherwood* had to be edited, as one of the scenes originally featured the character of the Sherriff of Nottingham having his head cut off and being revealed to be a cyborg. Two American journalists had recently been tragically murdered in a manner reminiscent of the scene, and the BBC therefore decided to make the cut.

- In order to achieve an appropriately lunar look for the episode *Kill the Moon*, which was largely set on the surface of Earth's satellite, the *Doctor Who* production team filmed in the rocky landscape of the Timanfaya National Park in Lanzarote, a country previously used as a location for the Peter Davison story *Planet of Fire*.

- Comedian Frank Skinner had been lobbying for a role in *Doctor Who* for some time before getting the part of engineer Perkins in *Mummy on the Orient Express*, and revealed on *The Jonathan Ross Show* that he had missed his child's second birthday in order to do the *Doctor Who* filming. The actor had even been watching the William Hartnell story *The Sensorites* when he got the call to read for the part!

- Some of the themes in the two-parter *Dark Water/Death in Heaven* caused offence to some viewers, with the suggestion that the souls of deceased people could experience the pain caused to their bodies when cremated. The BBC Complaints Department responded, saying that '*Doctor Who* is a family drama with a long tradition of tackling some of the more fundamental questions about life and death' and arguing that the themes explored were appropriate within the context of a science fiction programme, and that in any event the whole concept was nothing more than a scam perpetrated by the character of Missy.

- Steven Moffat attempted to keep the true identity of Missy secret for as long as possible. When key dialogue revealing who the character really was was recorded between Michelle Gomez and Capaldi during location filming outside St Paul's Cathedral, the actors whispered their lines and rerecorded them later. Moffat also had Gomez state she was a Random Access Neural Interface (RANI), so that fans would assume she was the renegade Time Lady previously portrayed by the late Kate O'Mara. The trick didn't really work, with Moffat commenting, 'Whenever I arrange skulduggery, no bugger notices.'

The adventure continues ...

A selection of Doctor Who web sites

www.bbc.co.uk/doctorwho
The official BBC *Doctor Who* website and the first port of call for information related to the programme. Includes clips, interviews, photographs and fun and games.

www.doctorwhomagazine.com
The website of *Doctor Who Magazine*, the four-weekly publication from Panini UK Ltd which has been running in one form or another since 1979.

www.gallifreybase.com
The most popular *Doctor Who* internet forum where fans share their views and discuss every conceivable aspect of the show. Highly addictive!

www.drwho-online.co.uk
A superb, fan-run website with all the latest news, reviews, interviews and competitions. A great source of information on the series.

www.dwasonline.co.uk
The *Doctor Who* Appreciation Society has been supporting the programme for nearly 40 years. Members receive a monthly newsletter and discounted prices on selected merchandise as well as special rates for *Doctor Who* related events run by the Society.

www.kasterborous.com
Kasterborous. Run by Christian Cawley and Brian A. Terranova, with a team of great *Doctor Who* fans providing news and reviews, bringing you honest and outspoken coverage of the world's longest running adventure series, with a touch of irreverence thrown in for good measure.

About the Authors

Will Hadcroft

Will Hadcroft watched *Doctor Who* avidly from the age of seven and became rather obsessed with it throughout the 1980s. He fantasised about being a writer like series scribe Terrance Dicks. He is the author of the *Anne Droyd* children's books, the young adult novel *The Blueprint*, and the *Mia* series for younger children.

His autobiography, *The Feeling's Unmutual*, was endorsed by *Tripods* trilogy author John Christopher and the Sixth Doctor himself, Colin Baker. Along with his writing, Will also runs FBS Publishing Ltd with Theresa Cutts.

Ian Wheeler

Ian Wheeler has contributed to books about *Doctor Who* and *Blake's 7* and has written widely about cult television. He was Coordinator of the *Doctor Who* Appreciation Society from 2001 to 2007 and has spoken about the series on television and radio.

He has written for publications as diverse as the *Financial Times*, *Best of British*, *Dreamwatch Bulletin*, *Comics International*, *CSO*, *Celestial Toyroom*, *TARDIS* and *Odeon Cinema Magazine*. In 2008, he won the Harrogate Advertiser Theakston's Old Peculiar Crime Writing Festival competition.

Lightning Source UK Ltd.
Milton Keynes UK
UKOW04f0356230215

246686UK00001B/2/P